THE DIARY OF PEACHES BROWNING

The world, close at hand and far away,
As seen by an intelligent labrador

Edited by
Thomas Carl Thomsen

Cross River Press * PO Box 473, Cross River, NY 10518 * 914 763-8050

THE DIARY OF PEACHES BROWNING
Copyright © by Thomas Carl Thomsen. All rights reserved. Printed in the United States of America. No part of this book may be used or reproduced in any manner whatsoever without written permission except in the case of brief quotations embodied in critical reviews or articles.

Library of Congress Cataloging in Publications Data.

First printing, May 1992

Thomsen, Thomas Carl 1920–
The Diary of Peaches Browning
by Thomas Carl Thomsen

p. cm

ISBN 0-945288-02-6

1. Dogs — Fiction I. Title
PS3570.H6464D5   1992
813′ .54—dc20

CIP 91-58927

*Dedicated to animal lovers
the world over*

Also by the author

Tales of Bequia, Cross River Press, 1988
Shingles, Cross River Press, 1990

Late spring, 1982

Dear Diary,

My name is Peaches and I am a yellow lab. I was born in a kennel in Ridgefield, Connecticut, this past winter. I was six weeks old when the Thomsens came to the kennels. They spent what seemed like an eternity looking over the litter, picking each of us up, examining us carefully. I remember the missus saying, "How can we choose just one when they all seem so cute." That was my cue. I began to jump up and down and I rolled over on my back and let my tongue hang out and I chased in circles as if to catch my tail. I thought to myself, "Please let this be enough 'cute'." It turned out to be just enough. The next I knew I was in their car and on the way to my new home.

I almost forgot to mention that there was a third party, a big, blond young man, who I learned later was my master's and mistress' son, Mike. I know he will never forget the ride home. I sat in his lap and had an accident.

I learned later that what sold them on me were my eyes, which are very large and, according to them, very glamorous. My lashes are very long and red. They named me Peaches after Peaches Browning, who I understand was a chorus girl in the thirties and was married to Daddy Browning, a multimillionaire who gave a lot of money away, particularly to pretty chorus girls. That was before he married Peaches. I learned this from my master and mistress.

When we arrived at my new home, I was greeted by a black and white spotted dog named Heidi. A dalmatian I learned later. We immediately took a shine to one another. She was older and not as frisky as I. I found out later that she had been Christian's dog at one time. I have heard a lot about Christian. He was my master's father and had lived with the family since his wife died many years ago.

I remember there was a dusting of snow on the ground when I was taken out with Heidi for my first walk. We went out back, where there is a very large pond. There were two geese on the shore and they looked at me with distain. I ran over to them, wanting to play. Heidi made no move and I quickly realized that they wanted no part of us. They flapped their wings and hissed at us. One tried to peck me. That's when I learned that with geese it's a good idea to stay your distance. I found out later that the two come to our pond every year at about this time. They have their routine. They build a nest on the side of the pond and not long afterward they appear on the pond leading a trail of tiny, fluffy, yellow goslings. My master's teenage granddaughter, Melanie, who lives with us, named them George and Tiffany. I don't know what significance the names have, except that at one time she had a boy friend named George. I understand that she has Tiffany tastes. Maybe that explains it.

I hope you are not having a problem grasping the fact that I am a dog and that I have developed a talent for expressing myself. I suppose it is a limited talent by peoples' standards. If you bear with me, I will try to make myself understood. Most people think that the only language we dogs have is body language. You know—wagging our tail, flopping our ears, extending our paw, and, of course, barking. I picked up what skill I have by eavesdropping on my master and mistress and occasionally watching television with them. Chanel 13 is my favorite.

We dogs have a different perspective from a human's. We're built lower to the ground, walk on four feet, don't pay taxes, and don't get into wars. We also have more knowledge than we are credited with. For example, when I joined the Thomsen family, I was aware that times were tough, that the country had a new and very popular president, and that a new movie opened up called "ET".

The way I see it is that if you can accept "ET", you really should not have any problem accepting me.
Because we are different, our perceptions of the world around us are likely to be different. In this diary I will try to record the goings on in this family and outside the family and the world at large from my perspective. I hope I am not being presumptuous in thinking that what I write may be of general interest. I am going to give it a try anyhow.

Early Summer, 1982

Dear Diary,

A few months have passed since I started this diary. It is going to be an occasional diary since I don't have the time to write on a regular basis.

Let me tell you a little about myself. I am not fully grown and I weigh about 50 pounds. I have been described as buxom. My master says he toyed with the idea of naming me "Dagmar", after a well endowed television personality who was very popular a few years back. I am glad they settled on Peaches, which is a much nicer name. My master and mistress agree that I am a peach of a dog. They get a kick out of telling friends how they came to pick that name.

It is summer now. Sometimes I lounge on the grass at the edge of the pond and listen to the flowers grow. But I would much rather run and fetch, which I understand is typical of my breed. Snooping around for something to eat is a good way to pass the time. I would love to get out and roam freely but that's a no-no. I love to fetch tennis balls. I could do that all day. But that is unlikely. Both my master and mistress have other things to do. Sometimes when I return the ball I don't give it up easily. I like to see them struggle to get it away from me. I can be mischievous at times. Pleasantly mischievous.

I like my life. I have a nice home. I am fed regularly. And I am loved. That is important. I love my master and mistress very much and it is nice to have my affection returned. They know that I love them. I follow them wherever they go. Park where they sit. Nudge them with my wet nose when they are watching TV. Wag my tail at every opportunity. I have a certain look in my eyes that tells them everything.

I don't want to give you the idea that everything is peaches and cream (pardon the pun). I am having a little difficulty with the housebreaking routine. My bed is in the laundry room. They put shredded paper on the floor, which I was supposed to use when I had to go. Unfortunately, I didn't get the hang of it as quickly as they expected me to. I got reprimanded when I had an accident and sometimes spanked with paper. The shredded paper has been removed and now I am taken out frequently during the day. But I am still having my problems. Nobody is perfect. Not even a lab.

I am wary of the pond behind the house. I understand Jumbie fell into the lake and later died. Jumbie was a black lab who belonged to Mike, my master's son. Jumbie loved to run. One day she impaled herself on a broken rake and fell into the pond. Mike got her to a hospital but she died during the night. I like to run, too, but I am careful where I run and I don't leap into the air. I think I am too chunky for that. I wouldn't say fat. Heidi also likes to run but she's not so agile. She's getting on in years. I can't say how old she is. I can't keep track of time like humans can. It just seems to flow on and on, until one day, I am told, it comes to an end.

There's another member of the family who I should have introduced earlier. He is a black and white cat named Snuf, which is short for Snufalufagus. Melanie named him when she was a child from a character in a children's TV show.

We all get along quite well—Heidi, Snuf and me. We sleep together, eat together and hang out together. It's like a kibbutz. But we have our differences. Snuf has his own ideas about exercise. He distains fetching, unless the object is a chipmunk. He is a pretty good hunter. To my mistress' chagrin, he likes to leave his catch at the door as a present, which does not go over so well.

I like the idea of doing this diary. I don't know of any other dog who has tried.

Summer, 1982.
Dear Diary,
What's a typical summer day like? Well, for one thing it is busy. I am still a pup and into everything. I love to explore, see new things, find new things, smell new smells, and chew things I am not supposed to chew. I guess that will change as I get older.

I love waking up. It is a thrill to see my master first thing. I get up on my hind legs, stretch as far as I can, and put my paws on his chest. He holds my head in his hands and gently rocks it from side to side. I love it.

First thing on my agenda and Heidi's is a quick walk. We can't waste any time getting outside because I am not completely housebroken as yet. Next is breakfast. I have learned to recognize the word "breakfast." When my master calls it, I know exactly what is meant and I respond quickly. After breakfast I find some toys to play with. Snuf also gets into the act with a ball that he chases around the living room. Heidi doesn't bother with that stuff. She acts like the grande dame. Now it is time for a nap. I find a place next to a window warm with sunlight and off I go in a matter of seconds.

Early in the afternoon I am taken out with Heidi for a good long run. We usually go into the woods behind the house. The variety of smells is tantalizing. I can tell where a rabbit has been, a racoon, a deer, even a turtle. I get very excited and run in circles trying to track the scents. My master watches carefully. If I leave his sight for just a second, he calls me back and I have learned to obey. I am bushed when we return and so it is another nap.

I have two meals a day and now I am ready for dinner. I get a combination of dog meal and canned meat and sometimes left-overs from the table. After dinner I park myself with my master and mistress when they read, listen to tapes, or watch

TV. I learn a lot by just being with them. A short walk before retiring is a must. Heidi and I turn in when they turn in. We sleep together on a big stuffed cushion in the laundry room. Snuff usually joins us.

Not a bad way to spend a summer day.

Late summer, 1982
Dear Diary,
  I love to lie on the grass at the edge of the pond and watch the animals around me. The squirrels and the chipmunks and the rabbits and the racoons and the ducks and the geese and the animals I cannot identify that swim across the pond with just their noses showing above water. Sometimes one of them gets close to me and tries to communicate. They all have languages. Grunts, groans, chirps, squeaks. I try to understand what they are saying but their language is over my head. At least for the present. Maybe when I get a little older I will understand. I hope so. They are living creatures and they have thoughts just like me and I bet they can be quite interesting.
  Thoughts like these were running through my head late yesterday afternoon when I must have fallen asleep. I dreamt I was visited by a squirrel and a chipmunk, who said they were from a place they called Animal Land. It was a very nice visit. They spoke glowingly about Animal Land. Apparently, everything works quite well there. It is peaceful and the animals seem quite happy. They have a council and an owl is in charge. He's a pretty smart bird. Seldom does anything go wrong, but if it does, he straightens it out quickly and fairly. He is very popular.
  A noise awakened me and when I opened my eyes, I saw the squirrel and the chipmunk perched on a log closeby. Maybe it wasn't a dream afterall.

Fall, 1982.

Dear Diary,

This is my first experience with fall. I didn't expect anything as colorful as this. The trees have turned yellow and red and the air is crisp. The smells are different, too. Sharper and more abundant. I am told winter lies ahead. I am familiar with that season. I like all the seasons. Each has something unusual and special about it.

Heidi, Snuf and I spend a lot of time together. Dogs and cats are not supposed to get along, so I guess we are special. When Heidi and I are taken out for walks, Snuf sometimes tags along. He actually heels. I don't think he knows that he is a cat. He embarrassed me a few nights ago. I was lying on the floor of the TV room, half asleep, when he came over and licked my face. I didn't know what to do at first. Then I decided to return the gesture. I licked his ear and he purred. Crazy.

I've told you about the animal members of the family but not about my mistress and master. My mistress is a very special person. She is beautiful and Mike says she was a knockout when she was younger. I think she still is. She is described as elegant by her female friends. What they mean, I guess, is that she has great poise and is very outgoing and really cares about people. She gets some kidding on this from her husband. Sometimes he addresses her as Madame Elegante. She says he is jealous, which he readily admits. He says that both can't be elegant. One has got to be down-to-earth. He describes himself as lean and mean. The mean part is a joke. He is anything but mean. He is very close to his family. Outsiders he deals with at arm's length, at least until he knows them well. That's the Swedish in him. I understand he is also part Danish, which is a totally different story. My mistress says that in some respects he is like his father, Christian, who was a poet and an inventor. She says he is also like his mother, who worked hard and was ambitious.

My master and mistress look very young for their ages. I am told that they met when they were eighteen and got married two years later. He likes to tell people he married an older woman—two days older. Sometimes I think his sense of humor is a little strange. His wife gave him an appropriate Valentines card a few months ago. On the cover it says, "There is something strange and wonderful about our relationship". When you open it up, it says, "You are strange and I am wonderful."

My master says the economy is beginning to improve. He says our new president is doing quite a job re-building pride and faith. I understand a new musical named "Cats" opened just the other night. Snuf ought to be interested. Do you suppose they will ever do a musical about labs?

Late fall, 1982

Dear Diary,
   My master says I am getting smarter. I am not sure what he is implying. I'm not completely housebroken yet. But I am becoming more observant. I know where the treats are kept and when it is time to eat and time to go to bed and a lot more.
   There was a concert on TV last night, which I watched with my master and mistress. At the end people in the audience showed their approval by slapping their hands together vigorously. Like they were after flies. It's called clapping, I understand. It was a funny sight. They looked like a bunch of penguins in dress clothes beating their wings together. Maybe you have noticed the way a flock of geese act when they are aroused? They flap their wings, stomp around, and make a terrible racket. I wonder how the habit of clapping got started. People have a lot of funny habits when you think about it. They sit on things they call chairs. Why not on the floor? They eat with tools they call knives and forks. A bowl would be simpler. Japanese drink out of bowls, just like dogs do. I guess dogs and Japanese are smarter. Look at the ridiculous clothes people make themselves wear. They don't look a bit comfortable, so why do they wear them? I have observed a trend towards less clothing among women. Their bathing suits aren't much bigger than a handkerchief. I suppose they are designed small so that they can be tucked into a perhaps bag. We dogs don't need a perhaps bag. We're ready to go anywhere, anytime, just as we are.
   Snuf thinks I am getting a little too precocious.

Winter, 1983

Dear Diary,

It is winter again. It is quite cold and snow is on the ground in abundance. I love the snow. I go wild in the snow. I love to run in the deep drifts and dig my muzzle into the snow banks. I don't mind the cold even when my muzzle is white with snow and ice. Hopefully, there is a fire in the fireplace when I come in. Curling up in front of a fire together with Heidi and Snuf is a great treat.

Just before Christmas we moved into a new house on the grounds of the country club. My master had worked on the new house for quite some time. He fancies himself a builder, although he is retired and building was never his trade anyhow. He seems to be busy all the time, so I wonder what he was like when he was not retired. I think it would be more correct to say that he did the contracting, rather than the actual building. He farmed out almost everything except some menial chores he could not hire anybody else to do. He says he saved a bundle by doing the contracting.

I am now a year old. My master and mistress had a birthday party for me. Everyone was there. My master and mistress, their children, Debbie and Mike, Deb's daughter, Melanie, who was home from school on a holiday and, of course, Heidi and Snuf. Melanie is affectionately known as princess. That goes back to a time when she was very young and my mistress bought a sign that said, "The princess is sleeping," and hung it on the door to her room. I think it has gone to her head.

It was my first birthday party and it was a blast. I got a number of presents—dog biscuits, a new collar, and a big cushion stuffed with cedar shavings. There were presents for Heidi and Snuf, too. Ordinarily, we are never fed from the table, but this was an exception and we all got goodies. I must have gorged myself because I felt a little uncomfortable later on.

It was a great party. I'll never forget it. In the middle of it Snuf started to purr. He has the loudest purr I have ever heard. It ought to be recorded.

The big news is that I am housebroken at last. It took quite some time and my backside became tender in the process. I don't know why it took so long. I understand certain breeds, like labs, take longer than other breeds. Considering the origin of our breed, it's probably not natural for labs to be housebroken in warm climates.

Not everything was peaches and cream (forgive me, I used that pun before). One day early this winter I was taken to the hospital. I didn't know why at the time because I was feeling fine. I was there all day. The doctor injected something into me and I blanked out. I came to a little later and felt quite groggy the rest of the day. When my master came for me, I heard the doctor say that the operation was a success and that my master would not have to worry about me having pups. I was surprised and shocked. I would have liked to have pups. It's a natural thing for a gal to have pups. It really wasn't fair to be denied the chance to have a family of my own. It might be different if I was undesirable. But I came from good stock and there's a good deal more to me than a pretty face. One day they will probably be sorry. Well, the deed is done and there's no point crying over it. I still love them both and I know they think that the operation was in my best interests.

They gave Heidi the chance to have pups when she was young and she produced a litter of fourteen. She and her pups were featured in a photograph on the first page of the Reporter Dispatch. Maybe that's why they had me spayed.

Late winter, 1983.
Dear Diary,
   This is a great location on the golf course. We've got quite a bit of property, so there is plenty of room to run around. Heidi and I have learned to recognize the split-rail fence that separates our property from the course. Sometimes very early in the morning or late in the afternoon my master will take Heidi and me for a run in the rough that parallels the 14th hole. Snuf may start out with us but he usually drops out. Heidi and I love to fetch but that is not Snuf's bag. Come to think of it, Heidi will give up long before I do. There are no golfers around when we go on our runs, so there have been no complaints. The location of our home has one disadvantage. My master has to wear a hard-hat to protect himself from stray golf balls when he cuts the lawn in the back.
   I like the red collar I got on my birthday a few months ago. There are several tags hanging from it. One is my ID. The other shows I have had a rabies shot and when it was given. Snuf also has a red collar, but it has a bell on it to warn chipmunks and squirrels. He never tires of chasing after them but he doesn't have much success anymore thanks to the bell. I am not sure that is fair. It is in his nature to hunt. It's the natural thing for him to do. On the other hand he doesn't hunt for food. Just for the sport of it. So, I guess belling him is fair after all.
   Mike is also a good hunter but he hunts for food for the table. Earlier this winter he brought home a deer which put extra meat on the table for his family for quite a long time. I understand he is a very careful hunter. He hunts with a bow and will not take a shot at a deer unless he is absolutely sure he will get it. He's also a good fisherman. He fishes with very light tackle to help even the odds. Last fall he hooked a thirty five pound striper on an eight pound line but couldn't bring

him in. That won't keep him from trying again. I guess that is the secret of success—to keep trying until you succeed.

I have heard my master tell about a stone monument he discovered in a deserted village in Massachusetts. On it was inscribed the saying, "Never try, never win." He was a young boy at the time. He's never forgotten it and he has tried to impress its meaning on Mike, Deb and Melanie. He likes to tell people that the inscription has helped him learn a lot about himself. What he can do. What he can't.

I have adopted some of his philosophy. I am very good at retrieving and I can catch a frisbee in mid-air, track a scent, open the cupboards in the kitchen, demonstrate my affection, and obey, well, most of the time. On the negative side, I don't like to swim and I am not a good watch dog. I have heard my mistress say that if a burglar entered the house I would give him my winning smile and then show him where the jewels are kept.

Fortunately, I have a winning personality. Everybody loves me. That's not surprising because I haven't found a person that I don't like. I am like my mistress in that respect.

I hear my master approaching. He is turning off the lights, which is his way of telling Heidi, Snuf and me that it is time to turn in. So be it.

Spring, 1983.

Dear Diary,

Melanie is home on a spring break from Rumsey Hall, a school in Washington, Connecticut. Melanie is Deb's daughter and right now she is living with us when she is not at school. She takes turns living with us and her mother. She is very bright and outgoing. My mistress says she is fifteen going on twenty one. A few days ago she brought home a boy who looked different from other boys. He was darker. She said he was black. He was the first black person that I had seen. He seemed very nice, pleasant. He patted me on the head as others have done and I liked it. I suspect that he was brought home to test the reactions of my master and mistress. Everyone seemed quite congenial and it turned out to be a very pleasant afternoon. I guess they passed the test because the boy wasn't brought back again to visit.

Dogs come in a variety of colors, too. I am a yellow lab. Jumbie was a black lab. Heidi is black and white. But color doesn't matter among dogs. We have our differences but they don't relate to color. I am not sure I understand why humans have a problem with color. Maybe it has been bred into them. I hope not.

My master has been able to rent out their house on Main Street, which is a relief. He had tried to sell it but there were no takers, so he rented it to a doctor from New Milford. After the papers were signed, he learned that the doctor had another residence in New Milford and that he planned to share the house on Main Street with his nurse. It seems that there is a fair amount of hankey-pankey in our community. Maybe it is the well water.

The family has expanded. It now includes two doves, presents from Debbie. They have quaint names—Archie and Mehitabel. One is pure white and the other is tan colored.

They live in a big cage in the atrium, which is just off the kitchen. It is glass-enclosed, loaded with plants and looks like a jungle. Before the birds arrived, Snuf spent a lot of time there basking in the sun, surrounded by exotic, sweet smelling plants. He looked pretty authentic in his jungle habitat. He is persona non grata in the atrium now.

The birds are allowed out of their cage quite frequently to fly about in the room. They are beautiful birds. Snuf agrees. They look yummy to him. One time he got into the atrium somehow. We heard a loud commotion coming from the birds. When my master arrived, Snuf was on top of the cage trying to get one of his paws inside. He was quite annoyed when he was removed from the room. I'm not sure our kibbutz can stand the addition of these two birds. They sure cramp Snuf's style and I'm not too keen about them. I don't suppose Deb would take them back.

Early summer, 1983

Dear Diary,

The trouble with learning by experience is that you frequently make mistakes. I made one a few days ago. I tangled with my first skunk. It was a very unpleasant experience. I saw this fascinating animal in the brush near our house. My intention was to make friends and to have fun. When I came close, he turned and squirted me with a foul-smelling spray. I gagged, shook my head, but couldn't get rid of the odor. I went home. My master instantly knew what had happened. He called a friend who told him to bathe me with tomato juice. He tied me up outside to keep me from getting in the house. He found several cans of tomato juice and proceeded to bathe me with the stuff. I think that was the worst thing that he could have done. The smell of the skunk spray was bad enough, but mixed with the tomato juice it was deadly. I became persona non grata. I was fed outside and that night I slept outside, the first time ever. The situation had not improved by next morning. I still smelled. Stank would be more accurate. By now my master realized that the tomato juice remedy hadn't worked and wouldn't work. He filled a big tub with water and gave me a bath with a disinfectant soap and then hosed me down. That helped a bit. Now the odor was all over him and he had to take a shower. Later in the day he gave me another bath. I spent another night tied up outdoors, which I really didn't mind so much. Heidi stayed her distance throughout. I guess she knew from her own experience what had happened and the best thing that she could do was not to get involved. Another bath, with a strong soap, after which I was let off the line, and I ran around the grounds and shook myself. The odor gradually disappeared and by the end of the third day I was let back into the house. I slept in the basement that night for the first time.

It was a terrible experience that I wouldn't wish on my worst enemy, if I had any. I guess all animals have their own defenses but that was pretty bad.

Summer, 1983.
Dear Diary,
The weather has turned quite warm and we desperately need rain.
The big event since I last wrote was Mike's marriage to Sarah. It was late spring when they got married in the local chapel, a landmark in Webatuck. There was a dusting of snow on the ground. Mike said afterwards that while he was waiting for his bride to appear he glanced out through one of the chapel windows and saw a brace of deer on the lawn, just standing, watching, curious. My mistress has a wonderful photograph of Sarah and Mike taken just after the wedding. Sarah is in heaven and Mike looks like a big, very happy puppy dog. The way I once looked, I guess. I am told that their reception at the country club was elegant. I should have been invited. I'm closer to Mike than many people who were invited. I bet there were some stray dogs around. I am just not considered when something important like this takes place.

Melanie is home from Rumsey Hall. I don't think she is very keen about the school. She is not so good with regulations. Apparently, there were many. I can sympathize. I like the idea of being free to run, to discover new things. I agree with Melanie that there are too many restrictions. But there's not much that I can do about it, except to complain.

We live adjacent to the tee on the fourteenth hole. The golf course is great. I am not supposed to be on it but I sneak out from time to time when no one is watching. We are not very far from Candlewood Lake, where my master took me a few days ago. We went early in the day before the mothers and children arrived. He was determined to teach me to swim. I am sorry to say that he failed miserably, miserably, miserably. I am not sure I will ever forgive him. At least not completely. He carried me out in the water and then dropped me in the lake. I was frantic. I paddled as fast as I could to get back to shore. It was a terrible, frightening experience. When I got ashore, I made a bee line for home. I didn't race. I just kept far enough ahead of my master so that he couldn't put a leash on me. He tried to explain to me when we got home that it was really important for me to learn to swim. Dogs can frown and if he looked closely enough, he would have seen one on my face. When he came close to me, I moved away. I kept my distance the rest of the day.

Late summer, 1983

Dear Diary,

This morning my mistress took me with her when she went shopping. I love to go for rides in the car. If we travel any distance, I like to put my head in her lap, and sometimes she strokes my head, which is soothing and may put me to sleep. I am not allowed in the car when my coat is shedding and getting into the new car is strictly taboo. I think that will change when the novelty of a new car wears off.

Everything looks different from a car's window. Trees, houses, people move by so swiftly you hardly get a chance to check them out. I like it when my mistress takes me grocery shopping. I am not allowed inside the store, which I think is a violation of some kind of right. Due process covers a lot of things. If she parks close enough I can smell the fresh-baked breads and when she brings her parcels to the car I get a chance to poke my nose into them. I can easily tell when she's been to the delicatessen counter, or the meat department, or the vegetable section. The smells are tantalizing. When we get home, I am usually rewarded with a dog biscuit. Why? I guess for being a good companion and guarding the car. I don't think I am a very good guard dog. I like people too much. That's the way we labs are. We're not fierce like dobermans. But if you want a lover, I am your kind of dog.

Late Fall, 1983

Dear Diary,

It is fall again and everything is as pretty as I remember it was this time last year.

Snuf tried to bring in a mouse this morning and was quite annoyed when it was taken away from him and discarded. He spent a lot of time looking for it but to no avail.

I like the chill of fall. When we come in after a run, my master will light the fireplace if it is cold enough, and Heidi, Snuf and I will curl up in front of it. Heidi looks positively regal stretched out on all fours, head aloft, in front of the fireplace. Snuf curls up next to me. What a cat!

I am not sure what I think about the invasion of Grenada. We certainly accomplished what we set out to do. We kicked the communists out, and that was good. But it was so easy. I get the impression that our president was looking for an opportunity to demonstrate that we are not pussy cats (sorry about that, Snuf), and this thing came along. I see the president tall in the saddle, charging up San Juan Hill. It's not San Juan hill, but you get the point, I think.

I heard my master and his son talk about hunting and the right to bear arms. I am told that in Animal Land the lions and elephants have taken a stand on hunting. Hunters come across the border from Hinterland and hunt for the sport of it and for ivory and skins. They are protected in Hinterland because their constitution allows them to bear arms. The constitution was written a long time ago when the country was young and living was perilsome and guns were needed to protect one's family. The lions and elephants say that guns are not needed in Animal Land, where the only danger is from hunters. They called a convention of animals and a resolution was passed outlawing guns and calling for fines and imprisonment for anyone breaking the law.

I told my master about this. He said there wasn't much chance of that happening here. We are all captives of the gun lobby, he said. I find that very strange.

I wonder if you have noticed that my interests are changing. A sure sign of maturity.

Winter, 1984.

Dear Diary,

Heidi and I went to stay with Mike while my master and mistress were away on winter vacation and Snuf visited Deb, who has four cats of her own. It's fun visiting with Mike and Sarah and their dog, Bear, who is appropriately named. I have never seen a bigger dog. Mike has to keep Bear on a lead. Except for yours truly and Heidi, he hates all other dogs. I think he considers them trespassers. We're family and that's different.

It was a great re-union when my master and mistress came back. I gave them my usual greeting. I jumped all over them and smooched. They looked well, tanned, and in great spirits.

My master had a battle with cancer and won. He's got chutzpah, a lot of it, more than his share of it. He says he's like the army air corps. "Nothing," he says, "can stop the army air corps, not even Mabel." I guess that was a saying in World War II.

From the way he tells it, that was the big war. Nothing phoney about that one, he says. It's strange how countries get into wars. Humans are supposed to be smart. I think we labs are smarter in some ways. I avoid fights. And that's not so difficult to do. The secret is to keep your cool and to use your head. I know I am known for looking glamorous. But I am not just a pretty face. There is also something inside.

Spring, 1984

Dear Diary,

Mike and Sarah celebrated their first wedding anniversary this spring and they did it appropriately by bringing their first child into this world on the same day. Her name is Chelsea. Sounds like an unusual name to me. I think it came from a popular movie.

Much as I like to run, fetch, play, and nap, there are moments when I prefer to cogitate. For a dog I am probably more inquisitive than others. For example, I have learned that there are 85 words in the Random House Dictionary that begin with 'dog.' I am sure that fact has some significance. But I cannot find any common thread that runs through the words. Their content varies widely. Some are slightly humorous, like 'doghouse.' Some are very serious like 'dogma' and 'dogmatist.' Many are very descriptive, such as 'dog days,' 'dog eat dog,' 'dog paddle,' 'dog watch.' There are many slang expressions that involve the use of the word 'dog.' For example: 'dog in the manger,' 'go to the dogs,' 'lead a dog's life,' 'let sleeping dogs lie,' 'put on the dog.' From these usages one could get very different concepts of what a dog is like. He could be nasty, or a loser, or withdrawn, or extravagant. I wonder how those slang expressions got started. I don't think any of them are descriptive of labs in any way. Incidentally, there are 74 words that begin with 'lab,' and 272 words that start with 'cat'. Snuf will be pleased to know that 'cat' is more popular than 'dog.' That's okay with me. Snuf is my kind of cat.

I wonder if my master is aware of the progress that I have been making in the learning department. He doesn't know about this diary and I am sure it will be quite a surprise when he does. Maybe I will give it to him as a birthday gift when I am older. Maybe on my tenth birthday, which is a long time away.

He may have some inkling that I am up to something. Sometimes when we are watching television he gives me the strangest look. Like he is puzzled. He likes to take my head in his hands and look into my eyes, nose to nose, or muzzle to muzzle, whichever, like he is trying to figure out what may be going on in my head. I wish I could tell him, but my speaking is limited to a few barks and groans. From the look on his face I can tell that he is on to something, that he suspects something is going on between the two of us that is unusual and not something he could discuss with anyone for fear he would be misunderstood and perhaps laughed at. Unfortunately, I can't help, at least not directly. I can give him my understanding smile, which he acknowledges with a pat on the head and a laugh.

Summer, 1984

Dear Diary,

I love the summer. I love all the seasons, but I am particularly fond of the summer months. I like the lazy feeling of lying on the cool, damp grass early in the morning and just looking around. This morning I was attracted by the sound of a bird in a tree closeby. His call was melodic and strong like he was trying to call attention to himself. Then I heard the response of another bird, maybe a hundred feet away. It was a sweet call. I listened carefully. The bird overhead was probably a male and he was trying to coax the other bird, a female, to pay him a visit. She was being coy like she was waiting for him to make the first move. The chatter went on for a while and then suddenly it ended. I think they flew off together. Thinking about them gave me a nice, warm feeling.

My master's cancer operation last winter does not seem to have affected his golf. He gets out once or twice a week. He and my mistress like to play the four holes next to our house in the evenings. They take just a few clubs and walk. It is surprising, he says, how well one can play with just a few clubs. I would like to go out with them but that's a no-no. So I wait for them on the patio. It only takes about an hour for them to play the four holes. When they return, I usually get my dinner. Heidi and Snuf, too. Of course, we have to listen to them re-play the four holes, but I don't mind. I like to see them in good spirits. Besides, when they play well, we usually get an extra treat.

I haven't been able to figure out the game as yet. It looks pretty simple. I guess the main attraction is the exercise. I think fetching is better exercise. Can you picture humans fetching? Or dogs golfing?

Melanie is home from school for the summer. She seems to be enjoying her vacation. She is taking up both tennis and golf and she is on the swim team at the country club. She's a good swimmer, just like her mother, Debbie, who, I am told, collected quite a few trophies growing up.

I'm not in their class. I haven't been able to figure out why I dislike the water. Dropping me in the lake didn't help matters. I don't go with them when they go for a swim in the lake. If I know they are going to the lake, I hide. I'm not really a coward. I know my limitations and I live within them.

Fall, 1984.

Dear Diary,

My master is quite a family man. I am told that when they lived in Knollwood there were four generations under one roof. His dad, Christian, his wife's parents, Mary and Jim, themselves, their children, Deb, Paul and Mike, and their granddaughter, Melanie. Now that's a kibbutz. Mike says it worked out fine. They had a big house and there was plenty of room for everybody. Five bedrooms with baths, two large living rooms, an enclosed heated porch which served as a third living room, and a cottage.

Their parents got along quite well. When people came to visit, they might find them in the garden, gently rocking, talking about their day, or just napping. It was Christian, my master's father, who held Mary's hand, as she lay dying.

I watch TV from time to time, when my master and mistress watch. Some of it is interesting but most is trash. That's what my master and mistress think and I agree. I do not know why it should be. My master says he has never been called on to give his opinions about TV programs and he doesn't know anybody who has.

I understand that they have tried to deal with this problem in Dumbo Land. Dumbo Land was once part of Animal Land but got kicked out, so my neighbor's dog tells me. He says there is a rating service in Dumbo Land called Nielsenwatch. The system works like this. There are a thousand or so sets that have been wired to record what programs are being watched. The sets are located in average hyena homes. On the basis of what the hyenas in these homes are watching, ratings are accorded every show and these ratings determine whether or not the show will continue. All of the other animals in Dumbo Land complain that with such a small universe it is no wonder that programs pander to the lowest denominator. The networks respond that the Nielsenwatch system is very democratic and reflects the true feelings and preferences of the public. Many complain that the networks should be able to come up with a system that takes everybody's interests and tastes into consideration. Then the quality would surely improve. The heads of the networks and the president of Nielsenwatch are also hyenas, so the complaint goes nowhere.

Some say that the problem will resolve itself in time. Standards will decline and sooner or later every animal will be watching the same program. Cultural correctness is the name of the game.

My master has been doing some writing recently. He's working on a book about Bequia, the island in the Caribbean that they visit from time to time. He says it is an enchanted island. I don't think I will ever get a chance to visit it. Dogs have to go through a quarantine in England for six months before they are let in. My master says that some of the French who visit the island should also go through quarantine first.

Winter, 1985

Dear Diary,

It is winter again and we are back at our Main Street house. I loved the house on the golf course but when the Main Street house did not sell, my master decided to put both houses on the market, and to live in the one that did not sell. As you might expect, our house on the golf course, which was smaller than this house and was supposed to be our retirement house, sold almost immediately.

My wish came true. The doves did not move with us. Heidi and I outvoted Snuf, who obviously had ulterior motives for wanting them to come along. Debbie found a nice home for them. I'm sure they will be happy and relieved that Snuf is not hovering about.

I am three now, which means that a big chunk of my life is behind me. It has been a busy and happy life so far. Come to think of it, I didn't have a birthday party this year. Nobody remembered. Not even me. I wonder what lies ahead. For me, Heidi, Snuf, my master and mistress.

There's a lot of glass in this house, so there are plenty of places to sit and look out. We frequently sit together, Heidi, Snuf and me. Our favorite spot is the living room, which has a glass wall facing the pond. There's ice on the pond now, and it's thick enough to go ice skating. I love to fetch on the ice. My master throws a ball. When I finally catch up with it, I can't put on the brakes and I slide a mile on my backside. Ever so often we have ice parties. My mistress invites a few friends over, they skate for a while, and then come indoors to sit by the big stone fireplace in the living room and gab. Although I am not supposed to mooch, I manage to inveigle a few treats. People like to stroke me and I like being stroked. I have been likened to a big teddy bear. That's okay with me.

What I like about my life is that there are relatively few restrictions. Few, that is, when compared with humans. I don't have to dress up for playing, eating, and sleeping. I can come as I am whatever the occasion may be. I don't have to sit at a table and be trapped into silly conversations in order to eat. I don't have to worry about making enough money to pay bills. I don't have bills. I don't have to pay taxes. I have a pretty good life, when you think about it, and I don't think I would like to change it in any respect, except to make it longer.

Freedom is great. It is the ultimate. It is really too bad that humans have surrounded themselves with restrictions. They say they have to in order to protect themselves from each other. That sounds kind of silly. Take away some of your freedom to enjoy the freedom you've got left? Crazy.

I wonder if people will ever change. Become more like us. Scientists are doing great things manipulating genes to produce better vegetables and fruits and livestock. I suppose there are serious risks if they apply their knowledge to homo sapiens. Super races might evolve and would they be white, yellow, red, black, or lavender? In what ways would they be superior? More intelligent? Stronger? More athletic? More aggressive? More reproductive? And who would decide? It's kind of scarey when you think about it.

There are also risks if they fool around with the genes of the likes of us. It is just possible that their efforts could lead to the development of superior animals with the talent to take over the world. Wouldn't that be a blast? It is kind of fun to consider the possibilities. I don't think we could do a poorer job of running things than humans have. Would I be a doctor, or a lawyer, or a chorus girl? One thing is for certain. I wouldn't be on a leash, and neither would my master or mistress be on a leash. We would all live together happily in one big kibbutz. Like we have now.

Having thoughts like these is a sure sign that I am getting older and, who knows, wiser?

Spring, 1985.

Dear Diary,

Thank God the winter is finally over. Ordinarily I like the cold, but we had a long siege of super-cold weather and a lot of snow. January was the worst. I think some kind of record was set for cold weather. At last the trees and shrubs are beginning to bud. Spring is in the air. I can smell it. I love the many different smells of spring. Welcome muskrats, beavers, ground hogs, foxes. Where have you been?

My master, The Master Builder, is back at it again. He has just started work on a cottage on the grounds for his son, Mike, his daughter-in-law, Sarah, their child, Chelsea, and Bear. He's like an Italian Don. He likes to have his family around him. I don't mind as long as I am included. Also Heidi and Snuf.

In that very cold month of January our president was inaugurated for a second term. If I recall correctly he was bareheaded. He's an interesting kind of guy. He likes to be photographed on a horse on his ranch out west. He's a cowboy at heart, and there's nothing wrong with that. My master says we have become too effete and need to get back to basics. Maybe our president can do that. We'll see.

There's one word he doesn't like and that is "quotas." He would have a real fit if he visited Dumbo Land. I know about Dumbo Land only from hearsay. A few of the dogs in my neighborhood have friends, who say friends of theirs have been there.

Dumbo Land has quotas on everything. The number of tennis balls you can fetch. The number of pups you can bring into this world. The number of treats you can have. The number of friends you are allowed to have. The hours of sleep you can have. The number of giraffes that can live next to gorillas. The number of monkeys who can be policemen and firemen.

It started out with quotas on jobs. It went on from there. Now it is promoted in a variety of ways. There's a commercial on TV, "Have you had your Quota today?" The government of Dumbo Land has its own version, "A Quota in every pot." Another, "Land of the free and home of the Quota."

I understand they have even installed a quota on the number of times you can vote in Dumbo Land. The politicians don't like that.

Our president recently came face to face with the problem. I understand he told Nancy that he would like eggs and bacon for breakfast. She had to remind him that he already had his quota of eggs for the week. I am told that he had a fit and blasted the liberals in Congress.

Summer, 1985.

Dear Diary,

Melanie turned sixteen a little while back. She had a sweet sixteen party and she invited a number of friends, including Heidi, Snuf and me. It was a blast. Lots of dancing, singing, jumping around, smooching. It's strange how wound up kids become when they get together and there aren't any adults around. Like they've just been released from prison. If dogs and cats behaved like that, we'd be put in cages.

I think the word for Melanie is irrepressible. She's like my master. They both think they can do everything. Melanie attended the New York Military Academy this past year. My Master tried to talk her out of going. He asked her why she wanted to go. She said the Academy had horses and that she would also learn to fly. Later my master found out the real reason. The ratio of male to female cadets is about ten to one.

The house my master is building for Mike and Sarah has been framed. It looks great. It has a long, wide porch along the front and a high roof. Mike and Sarah can't wait to get in. They're living with her folks for the present, which is fine. But they want their own place and that is natural.

The geese came back this spring and produced five gosslings. I think there were six at the beginning but there's a big, nasty turtle in the pond who, I think, got one of them. The parents try to be protective. Papa leads the way as they swim in single file and Mama is on guard at the rear. They are yellow when they are born and don't begin to look like geese until much later. They are gone now. Once they learn to fly they take off. I think they come back to visit during the summer, but I am not sure that I can recognize them. Once grown all geese look alike.

An astonishing fact about geese. They mate for life. They are like humans in that respect. I wonder how it came to be.

There are some good sized bass in the pond. Mike loves to fish. My Master got a dingy for the pond, which Mike uses to fish. He hooked a big one a few days ago. He said it was at least five pounds. Chelsea also fishes at the edge of the pond for sunfish.

Summer days are the best. The grass is cool in the shade alongside the pond. I like to watch what goes on. There's some kind of animal that swims across the pond from time to time, with only its nose showing out of water. Mike says it is a beaver. We have many deer around but you see them mostly in the fall and winter when they come out of hiding to scavenge for food. Last winter my master put a bale of hay in the woods behind the house for them to eat. But they wouldn't touch it. Then someone told him it had to be green to attract them, so he sprayed it with a green vegetable dye, but that didn't work. He read that deer like apple mash and he called a local orchard to find out if he could buy left over apple mash, but they were discouraging. Finally, he gave up the idea of feeding the deer. I don't think he gave up the idea permanently. It's not in his nature to give up.

Melanie's mother, Debbie, is as busy as ever. She's a nurse and there is plenty of work for her. I understand that her husband took off many years ago, when Melanie was quite young. She and Melanie lived with my master and mistress on and off in the years that followed. They had their own cottage when they lived on Knollwood. At one time it was a chicken-coop which my master, together with his dad, Christian, converted into a cottage. My master and his dad worked quite well together. They built a two-horse stable next to the garage for Deb's horse and for his own. I am told that my master was not a particularly good rider but he did his best. Part of his philosophy: "Never try, never win." He got thrown a couple of times, once in Arizona, when he broke a couple of ribs.

Still he didn't give up. He got back on the horse before they left for home. Melanie was with them then. She fell, too, and got back on her horse. I haven't heard either of them talk about riding recently, so I guess they've finally given up on riding. Smart.

His "nothing can stop me" philosophy is okay but you can carry it too far. Nothing in the world could persuade me to take a dip in the lake. Nothing.

Fall 1985.

Dear Diary,

Mike's and Sarah's cottage is coming along nicely. It is completely enclosed. I understand it will go more slowly now. They tell me their target date is next summer. I think they are expecting another member of the family about that time.

I saw Mike and Sarah sitting on the front porch on rockers this afternoon, making believe the house had been completed and that they had moved in. They just rocked and rocked and smiled contentedly. I wandered over and sat between them and listened to the squeaking of the rocking chairs. Heidi didn't come along. I think she was napping. I have no idea where Snuf was. Probably chasing a chipmunk.

Mike's got a big pile of logs stacked on the ground between the cottage and Main Street. I heard him tell Sarah that he plans to cut them in two foot lengths and split them and sell them as firewood. He is trying to make a go of his landscaping business, which he started a few years back. He's got plenty of customers but some are slow in paying their bills. Apparently there is an inverse ratio between affluence and paying bills promptly. Strange.

The logs are a little unsightly. I hope the neighbors don't object. They won't be there long. He's figuring on cutting about fifty cords, and most are already sold.

I understand that my master and mistress are planning to visit Bequia again this winter. My master has been collecting information about Bequia and is planning to write a book.

Mike brought Bear with him today. He's a great big dog. Looks like a Newfie. That's short for Newfoundlander. He went around the property and marked it out in the usual male dog manner. I don't think he missed a bush. Only males do this. I don't know why females don't. Don't want to intrude on the male's domain, I guess. That will change for sure.

Winter, 1986
Dear Diary,
In a few days my master and mistress will be off for Bequia on holiday. I really don't mind. Staying with Bear will be a treat.

There was a program on TV last night about lawyers. According to the program, lawyers are now permitted to advertise. I think we are far behind Dumbo Land, where, I understand, lawyers have been allowed to advertise for quite some time. I have written about Dumbo Land before. It is kind of a far out place. From what my friends tell me, Dumbo Land is well advanced in the art of using advertising to promote legal services. It is fairly common to see advertisements in the subways and on the sides of buses and on throwaways tucked into an A & P circular. Negligence lawyers are pretty aggressive running their advertisements on the sides of ambulances. It is not unusual to see compelling messages scribbled across the sky. The advertisement I like best is the lawyer photographed in the robes of a judge. The headline reads, "Justice for all at prices you can afford."

One of our neighbor's dogs has been in touch with a pal in Dumbo Land. The news is that there is great excitement over the introduction of fragrances for both female and male animals. This is a very new thing. Animals are not accustomed to using fragrances, at least not in Animal Land. Dumbo Land is another matter. As I wrote, the animals in Dumbo Land are kind of weird.

Well, the manufacturers are pretty clever. One has come up with some exotic names, like Provacateur and Promiscuous. Another manufacturer has a somewhat different approach. He's named his perfumes Hemlock and Chloraform. The rage now is to come out with fragrances designed for specific breeds. Dances with Dobermans is very popular. Zebras go for Stripes. Sleep with a Lion has its obvious appeal. The hoi polloi go for Animal, which has broad appeal. High on the totem pole of those low on the totem pole is Copulate. I think that is pretty vulgar and should be banned. There's an idea! A fragrance named Banned. That should be popular.

I go for the outdoor smells myself, not the stuff you spray on. I'm a lover but I like to be au natural.

Spring, 1986

Dear Diary,

Well, they went away to Bequia again this past winter and came home looking tanned and refreshed. My master has been very busy working on his book about Bequia. I understand the theme is that Bequia is an enchanted island and has a magical effect on many people who come to it in search of escape, paradise, a new life. My master has developed ten case histories to prove his point.

I would like to visit Bequia. My master says dogs have to go through quarantine in England for six months before they are allowed into Bequia. That's not fair. Talk about discrimination.

Mike's cottage is just about completed and Sarah, Mike, Chelsea and Bear are about ready to move in. Sarah is pregnant but you can hardly tell. She must be carrying it in some unusual place.

I've been through the cottage. I followed Mike around one day. It's kind of small but neat. On the main floor there is a living room with a cathedral ceiling and two bedrooms and a bath. On the lower level a kitchen and dining area. The attic is unfinished but it could have two more bedrooms and a bath. Mike and Sarah are very excited about their new home. So is my master, The Master Builder. Bear is also looking forward to moving in. It will be great having Bear as a neighbor.

My master and mistress have been talking about animal rights with their friends and neighbors. They received some literature recently from an organization in the midwest describing various animal abuses. They were very upset by what they read. Chickens being warehoused in tiny cages until they are fattened up and ready for slaughter. They never get out of their cages until the end. Calves and other animals are handled in the same way. Living comfortably as I do, I have never given any thought to this kind of thing until now. It is really appalling when you realize that the only rights that animals have are those that a few have won in their struggle for survival. I mean wild animals like tigers and lions. Animals that have been domesticated are completely subservient and must bend to the wishes of those in control.

I have a very good life by comparison, but the point is that I am lucky. There are so many other animals and species of animals that are not as lucky. Cows and chickens, for example. They are raised solely for the purpose of providing meat on the table. They have absolutely no say in the matter. They are living creatures and are entitled to their lives and to do with them as they please, not as somebody else pleases. Horses are somewhat better off, at least the ones who aren't slaughtered for dog food. The lucky ones have the chance to race their hearts out to make money for their owners, or to provide entertainment and exercise for their riders. I don't think that is fair. Why shouldn't they have some voice in the matter?

Horses are bred primarily to run. Maybe the singularity of their breeding is the reason why they are not very bright and are easily controlled and manipulated. I am glad I am not a human. I would have a great deal of trouble imposing my will on other creatures. But that seems to be characteristic of humans, controlling others and forcing them to do their bidding. On their own kind, too.

I have silly dreams from time to time, just like humans. In one of them the roles of humans and animals are reversed. Humans run at the race track and the winner is awarded with a flowered wreath that is hung around his neck. That's kind of funny. Not so funny is a stock yard filled with grunting humans not realizing the fate that awaits them. There's one dream that is very upsetting. I see a row of cages four by four and eight high and in each one is a naked human whose life is limited to eating and sleeping standing up. Ugh!

I like the way that dream ends. A dalmatian rides by on a fire truck and opens up all the cages and the humans are freed. I think the dalmatian is Heidi. She's some dog!

Summer, 1986

Dear Diary,

The cottage has been completed and Mike, Sarah, Chelsea, and their dog, Bear, have moved in. They are ecstatic. Mike says it's the most important thing that has happened in his life. They had a little party. Champagne and some goodies were served. I popped in. Heidi didn't show. She's doing a lot of sleeping these days. I guess it's the heat, although she's beginning to show her age. Snuf hung around outside for a while but didn't come in. He stays his distance from Bear. Bear wouldn't hurt him but his size is intimidating. Mike had tears in his eyes when he thanked his mother and dad. They were moved too. It was a very nice occasion.

A few weeks after the housewarming Sarah added to the Thomsen population. She brought Jordan into the world. Sarah is amazing. Only a week before delivery she was going to her aerobics class and doing her usual exercises. It was hard to tell that she was pregnant. You'd think a thin person would show, but not Sarah.

I have become aware of a daily ritual that puzzles me. I can see the road from one of my favorite spots near the pond. There's a steady stream of cars going down Main Street in the morning and then in the opposite direction at the end of the day. My master isn't involved in this ritual but most of our neighbors are. He tells me that he isn't involved because he is retired. It's a funny routine. They're back at where they started, the day is gone, they look pretty beat, and they're met at the door by a tired wife and a bumptious kid. We animals are much better off. We are not slaves. We can run when we want to, play when we want to, sleep when we want to, and we don't have to go to work. When you think of it, we have a pretty good life.

It's a nice warm summer day. Heidi is resting on the lawn in front of the pond. I see Snuf trying to catch a frog. A couple of days ago he fell into the pond trying to catch a frog. Boy did he move! It's too nice a day to sit inside and write. I think I will join them.

Fall, 1986.
Dear Diary,
A dreadful thing has happened. My master got shingles and he's in the hospital. Mistress says he's in terrible pain. His face is blown up and distorted. She says he looks like elephant man. I understand elephant man was a poor disfigured wretch who wandered about in the English countryside in the late 1800s. His face was lopsided and ugly and scarey.

The doctor put him in the hospital immediately because he was afraid that the virus would attack his eye and cause blindness. He'll be there until they get the infection under control.

Everybody is quite concerned. The surgeon, who did his cancer operation a few years back, popped into his hospital room to visit and was aghast. He said it was the worst case of shingles he had ever seen.

I'm lucky. I haven't had a sick day since I was born. So, I really don't know what it is like to be sick. I think humans are more vulnerable to illnesses than dogs. We must have a better immune system.

On a different subject, I am told that there is trouble brewing in Animal Land. It seems certain animals are upset because they are not doing as well as everybody else. Dobermans are causing most of the trouble. They want special attention and privileges on the grounds that they haven't been around very long and consequently haven't accumulated very much of anything. They think they are entitled and that affirmative action should be taken to help them. They appealed to the chief, who is a wise, old owl. Very politely the owl suggested that if they worked hard, they would be able to catch up. They responded that would take forever and they wanted their due now. Affirmative action is the only answer, they said. The owl met with his council and then came back with a plan. He told them about Dumbo Land. He said that affirmative action was the rage there and he announced that Animal Land would provide free passage for any doberman who wanted to migrate to Dumbo Land.

It's my guess that a lot of the dobermans will take up the owl's offer. I hope so.

Late fall, 1986.

Dear Diary,

What a time my master is having with shingles. He has been in the hospital again, this time because the pain was so bad that he could not handle it with the usual pain killers. He was in the hospital for eight days the first time and ten days the second time. When he came out the second time, the doctor put him back on oral medications, which haven't worked so well. He is in considerable pain most of the time. He says that managing cancer was a breeze by comparison.

He went to the library and the local bookstore looking for information on shingles, but wasn't successful. Now he's going through the files of the medical library at the hospital. One thing about my master. He's persistent.

There was a feature on TV last night about the high salaries paid to sports personalities. Highest was $4 million. I can't recall his name. That hardly matters. I was surprised to learn that one of the TV anchor men gets $1.4 million. By comparison the president of our country gets about $200,000, I think. Maybe Reagan can get a job as a TV anchor man when he retires from office. I think he's probably too old to take up golf seriously. A past president tried his hand at golf, but he stumbled a lot and occasionally drove his golf ball into the spectators. Reagan sits pretty well in the saddle. Maybe he could be the wrangler at a dude ranch retirement home.

Winter, 1987
Dear Diary,
We had a very big snow last night. Mike bought a plow a few weeks back and last night he fastened it to his truck. He was up long before dawn to start plowing. He worked until late in the afternoon, returned, and flopped into bed for a few hours sleep before going out again.
My master is still suffering from shingles. He's taking various kinds of medication for the terrible pains in his forehead and around his right eye. He looks kind of beat. He has collected a great deal of information about shingles and has decided to write a book to share what he has learned with fellow sufferers.
There are many wild animals in the neighborhood—deer, raccoons, possums, beavers, snakes, ground hogs, to mention a few. I had an interesting visitor yesterday, a silver fox, who said he was from Animal Land. He was different from most silver foxes that I have met. He seemed pretty normal. None of the clannish mannerisms that you usually associate with silver foxes. He didn't wear a beanie and his long tail wasn't braided.
We had a very interesting conversation. He said that many silver foxes in Animal Land felt they were being ostracized by other animals, and that they were not being given the recognition they were entitled to by virtue of their many contributions in such fields as commerce, law, medicine, and entertainment. Frequently they are the targets of criticism and abuse. It seems that anytime something goes wrong in Animal Land they are blamed. The foxes' leader confronted the owl who runs things in Animal Land. He was quite direct and outspoken. He said to the owl that foxes are treated like second class citizens. "I don't think I will ever see the day when a fox will be elected to the presidency of Animal Land," he said.

The owl and his council thought about this for quite a while and then summoned a delegation of foxes for a meeting. The owl said that the council had determined that the foxes were largely responsible for their own predicament. He said that many were clannish, preferring the company of their own kind to that of their fellow animals. Foxes, he said, work very hard at maintaining their own culture and dealing with others at arm's length.

At first the foxes strongly resented the criticism. But the more they thought about it, the clearer it became that the owl was right. The foxes' leader then asked the owl and council what they should do. The owl responded quickly and forthrightly. "Drop the idioms and mannerisms of your ancestors and assimilate yourself into the ways of Animal Land. Frankly, you draw attention to yourselves with your beanies and braided tails. All of us here are originally from other lands and different cultures and we have been able to fit in. You can, too, if you want to."

The foxes went back to their dens and thought about the advice they had been given.

The silver fox looked me over carefully to check my reaction. He said he wasn't sure how many foxes would follow the owl's advice. "It's very difficult," he said, "to break tradition. But I think the owl is right. I have started to change my ways. Do I look or sound different from the other foxes you know?" I told him that I thought he was quite different and that we should become good friends. He was very pleased. "I may even be welcome in the hen house," he said and departed.

Spring, 1987

Dear Diary,

I wish I could enjoy this fine spring weather more, but Heidi is not well. My master has had her to the vet several times recently. He prescribes medications that seem to rejuvenate her, but the results are not long lasting. She sleeps a lot by the window in the living room in the warm sunlight. I think her problem is mainly age. I am very concerned but I do not know of anything that I can do, except to sit with her and try to comfort her. I feel helpless and dread what may lie ahead.

Melanie has a beau, a nice looking young man named Pedro who hails from Portugal. She is seeing quite a bit of him. Looks like it may be serious. She seems radiant and very happy. Isn't love wonderful?

My master is spending a lot of time at the New York Academy of Medicine collecting information for his book on shingles. I heard him say that he is such a frequent visitor that they greet him as doctor when he arrives at the library, and when he leaves the doorman asks if the doctor would like a cab. He says it is a Walter Mitty experience. I am not sure I know what kind of an experience that is, but I will let it pass. Even a lab can't be expected to know everything.

I think you know that I watch TV from time to time with my master and mistress. Not too much. It can become habit forming and divert you from more important things. Like watching the sun shining through the trees and creating patterns on the grass glistening with morning dew. Or watching Snuf trying to catch a chipmunk. Or visiting with Heidi who seems so sad.

Last night there was a program about the efforts of astronomers to discover the beginnings of the universe. It was fascinating. There is a theory that it began with a big bang and from this explosion evolved millions of galaxies like our own. It was exciting but then the thought crossed my mind what practical purpose could be behind such an effort, which is taking the time of many scientists and costing millions of dollars, maybe billions. When they find the answer, will they be able to alter the course of events? Of course not. Our world will be no different from what it is today. We will continue to be devastated by catastrophic storms, droughts, plagues, famines, disease, wars. The inequities and deprivations that exist today will continue to exist. Right? We won't be any worse off, true, but neither will we be any better off. So what's the point?

Don't misunderstand me. I am not against learning more about our beginnings. Maybe we will find out how dogs and cats and birds and other animals fell behind in the struggle of the fittest for survival. It would be interesting but it wouldn't have any bearing on our status today as lesser creatures.

I guess it is really a matter of priorities. There are many serious problems that need to be addressed and these should take precedence. I really think that if labs were in charge, a far greater effort would be directed at finding answers to famines and diseases and the homeless and the inequities that separate the have-nots from the haves. If not dogs, then some other species. Monkeys are supposed to be fairly intelligent. They lost out in the battle of evolution. Maybe they should be given another chance. I get thoughts like this when I lie out in the baking sun too long. I sure don't like the thought of sitting at the foot of some blithering monkey.

Summer, 1987

Dear Diary,

I've got good news and bad news to report. The bad news is that Heidi died. Her health went downhill very rapidly this past winter. She had great trouble just walking and spent most of her time sleeping in the sun. The vet said that she was in pain and that the humane thing to do was to put her to sleep. My master agonized over the problem. But he felt there really was no alternative, and so he consented.

The vet came up to the house. My master and mistress sat with Heidi on the floor of the living room next to her favorite window. My master held her head in his lap and my mistress stroked her as the vet administered something into her body and in seconds she was gone. She passed very quietly and I remember the tears in my master's and mistress' eyes. She had been a very important part of the family for many years and it hurt deeply to have her go.

This was my first encounter with death. I sat closeby and just looked. She did not seem to be in pain. She just looked up at her master and mistress, her eyes filled with love and trust. I was very moved by the experience. Her life was gone and it happened so quickly and quietly. Years of living, of happiness and excitement and love just ended. I wonder if she knew what was about to happen. Perhaps she was grateful. When my time comes I do not know how I will act. At this moment I know I will not want my life to slip away but to continue forever.

My master and mistress cried as they buried her in the garden next to the pond. I did not go outside with them. I watched from the picture window in the living room. I felt very sad. As I watched, I realized that I would never see her again, run with her again, play with her again, sleep with her again. The ending of life is so final and incomprehensible. Emotions welled up inside me that wanted to come out but were trapped. If I could cry like a human, I think that would have helped. But my tears were inside.

Now the good news. Melanie got married. I remember it was a beautiful morning. Melanie had been up for hours getting ready for the big event. She looked very radiant, happy, and beautiful. Deb had stayed overnight to help with last minute arrangements. At about nine a great big white limousine pulled up in front of the house and Melanie, her bridesmaid, her mom, and my master got in. I understand that the limousine almost broke down on the way to the church at Good Counsel in White Plains, where her mother had gone to school. The car choked and balked and for a moment it looked like they would have to walk the remaining mile or so. But it revived and managed to reach the church huffing and puffing and, of course, late.

From what everyone has said, it was a great wedding. Deb had made most of the arrangements since my master and mistress were away when the news of her pending marriage broke. She found a priest who spoke Portugese and at the end of the ceremony he gave a short talk in Portugese mainly for the benefit of Pedro's parents who flew over for the occasion. My master gave her away. Reluctantly, I am told. Reluctantly, because she had been more like a daughter to him than a granddaughter.

Nobody invited me to the wedding or to the reception. It was quite a reception, I understand. It was very spirited, as you can imagine with well over half of the hundred plus celebrants being Portugese. There was a lot of toasting. My master set the pace. First he toasted the bride and groom, then Melanie's mom, next Pedro's parents, members of the wedding party and finally all of the Portugese assembled. Dear Chelsea, now three, took the cue. She got up on a chair, lifted her glass and toasted the "broom."

After the wedding the bride and groom took off to Club

Med in Florida, where they spent their honeymoon. I wasn't invited to go along, and I wasn't invited to the rehearsal dinner the night before at the country club. I am beginning to feel overlooked.

Fall, 1987

Dear Diary,

I was lying on the grass near the pond not doing much, just observing, when I noticed a rather large turtle emerge from the pond and slowly crawl along the ground until it reached a very large flat rock at the edge of the pond. It climbed on top of the rock and began to sun itself, which I thought was unusual. The turtle didn't move at all. It seemed completely relaxed, with head and legs fully extended. If he knew I was there, he did not seem to mind. I thought that is the way animals should be, relaxed and unafraid.

I like to watch what goes on around me and I can sit watching for a long, long while, even hours. There is always something to be learned by observing life around you. There is a message if you watch and listen carefully to the birds and bees and squirrels and chipmunks and turtles and maybe even the fish in the pond.

At that moment a squirrel came on the scene. He looked me over carefully and then shifted his gaze from side to side, as though looking for something. Probably making sure Snuf was not around, I thought.

The squirrel collected a few nuts and carried them in the pouch of his mouth close to where I was lying and began to eat. He saw the turtle but did not pay him much heed. Obviously, I posed no threat to him. I liked that.

A short while later a silver fox showed up. It turned out to be the same fox I had met a few months back. He said he was glad to see me again, and I returned the compliment. He said that he was pleased to report that the fox situation on Animal Land was beginning to resolve itself, as more and more of his brethren were dropping their old ways and acclimating themselves to the culture of Animal Land.

"We had a bit of a scare a few weeks ago," the fox said, as

he swished his bushy tail to show it was no longer braided. "A bunch of dobermans from Dumbo Land slipped across the border into Animal Land and raised a terrible ruckus at several movie houses where a film was being shown about animal equality. The outrage was brought to the attention of the wise owl, who, you know, runs things on Animal Land. Reminded of the way the French government handled troublemaking emigres from Africa, the owl ordered the immediate deportation of the offenders to Dumbo Land."

"A wise move," I said.

"I am glad you agree," the fox said. "Incidentally, I am here on a mission. I am officially an emissary from Animal Land now and it is my assignment to spread the gospel."

"What gospel?" I asked.

"Peace, love, respect, kindness," he said.

"Congratulations," I said. "I wish you every success."

The fox left. The squirrel followed him with his eyes until he was out of sight and then resumed feeding himself.

"Must be a leftover hippy from the sixties," the turtle said and scampered back into the pond.

Late fall, 1987

Dear Diary,

It looks like we are going to be moving again. Most families, I am told, stay put for ten or so years. Not this one. I think my master has an on-going case of itchy feet. He finally sold this house on Main Street and we should be moving to Adams Farm before the snow starts to fall. He tried to sell this house about four years ago, but there weren't any takers at the time. I understand the real estate market is much improved. It may not stay that way for long, considering the recent debacle on Wall Street. My master has his fingers crossed. If all goes according to plan, we'll move early in December, Mike will move to New Fairfield, Connecticut, and Deb to a condo in Brewster. Melanie is not involved in any move. She and Pedro have an apartment on Lake Mahopac. They moved to the lake when they came back from their honeymoon.

Melanie looks very happy. It's wonderful what love can accomplish. Humans make quite a ritual out of love and marriage. We dogs don't have anything comparable. We mate without any ceremony and a few months later we give birth. I think it is interesting the routine that nature has laid out for humans. Unlike us you can mate frequently, which I suppose was designed for the purpose of developing an on-going bond between the male and female. A pretty nifty device, you might say, for keeping them together with their offspring. Without such a bond, there would be no society of the sort that exists now. I wonder how it came to pass that nature confined this pattern to humans. Do you suppose it was like this from the very beginning? Or did it develop over time? And if that is the case, why was it confined to humans? Why were they favored? Why not animals. Like labs. I think this needs exploring.

Christmas, 1987.

Dear Diary,

It has been a very nice Christmas. Christmas Eve we had smorgasbord, which is traditional in our family, and after that we opened our presents. I got a box of treats and Snuf a new pillow for sleeping. Mike and Sarah, and their two children, Chelsea and Jordan, were present. Also Deb and Melanie and Pedro, and, of course, my mistress, and the chief, as he now likes to call himself. There were many presents and lots of excitement and the living room was alive with joy and the floor was littered with wrappings. The only sad note was Heidi's absence. It was the first Christmas without her. I miss her a great deal.

We celebrated Christmas at our new home on Adams Farm, which is also in Webetuck. The sale of our Main Street house finally went through, although at one point it looked as though it was going to fall apart. I was sorry to leave Main Street. I liked its location on the pond and the woods around it. I have a lot of memories tied in with that house. I am thinking particularly of Heidi and the lovely times we had together. I guess you are getting on when you begin to collect memories.

A few nights ago we were watching a TV program about race relations when I fell asleep and had a strange dream. The dream was about a breed of dog that originally came from some remote part of the world. It wasn't a razor back, or any breed that I'd seen before. It was big, muscular, very agile, like a cross between a bear and a doberman. The breed was having great problems adjusting to the other animals in the community. Apparently it resisted training. Some said the breed was having problems because it was disadvantaged and poor. An Irish Setter, who had been trained as an anthropologist, explained that while other breeds had succeeded in being assimilated, this breed would take longer to assimilate because it had only recently emerged from the wild and had not yet developed the skills that would allow it to adapt and grow. He was very pessimistic and said it might take many years before it had acquired the ability to exist on an equal footing with other animals. His statements caused an uproar. It seemed that no one wanted to hear what he had to say. Most took an opposite position and felt that with special allowances and a good education the breed would be able to catch up. Many said it was the fault of society for having deprived the breed of the skills that other animals had developed successfully. There was talk of setting up a special school with a curriculum designed to help the breed mature and become responsible citizens. The proponent was called a segregationist and was asked to leave. At this point in my dream doors suddenly opened and a swarm of dogs of this breed burst into the hall and took over. Their leader took to the rostrum and labeled everyone in the room racists, even their most ardent supporters. Of course, they weren't racists. They were mostly dogs just like me. The intruders barked a lot, jumped around, and sang and rapped in weird cadences. The other animals were careful not to offend. They listened and watched and after a while they were caught up in the frenzy and many joined in the rapping. The sounds and rhythms were kind of weird. I had never heard them before. They were catchy and they spread quickly throughout the community and in time it became politically correct not to criticize this new breed. It was reasoned that basically they were like other animals and in time differences would disappear. As it turned out, the observation was partly right. The breed didn't change, but the rest of the animals adapted to their ways. It was a strange dream. I couldn't get it out of my mind.

Early winter, 1988

Dear Diary,

    Mike took Bear and me out hunting a few weeks ago. I was staying with Mike while my master and mistress were away.

    It was exciting and quite dangerous. He took us out in an open field near where he lives in Connecticut. We were hunting for birds, which I had never done before. I remember it was very early in the morning and there was snow on the ground. All of a sudden I got the scent and instinctively I pointed. A bird flew out of the tall grass right at me. I was startled. I must have jumped a couple of feet off the ground. I heard a shot and I felt pellets whiz by over my head. I panicked and ran back to Mike. He laughed and patted me on the head. That was enough hunting for me. I stayed very close to him and let Bear do the hunting the rest of the morning. He was pretty good at it. I really didn't mind. We are all good at something and hunting obviously is not my cup of tea. I like that expression. Sounds kind of British.

    We did not go out hunting again. But Mike took us on nice long walks in the woods and let us run free. That was great. One day we walked down to Candlewood Lake. I didn't go close to the lake. Water is not for me. Call me a pussy cat. On second thought Snuf would object.

    Mike has two great kids, Chelsea and Jordan. I love kids. I love to play with them. Jordan climbs on top of me as though I am a horse. She's only two but quite heavy. Bear is much bigger and stronger than I and can carry Chelsea, who is four, with ease. The kids are both very blond like their father. I am surprised because Sarah's hair is quite dark. Sarah is a heck of a mother. She is there for them all the time. It is not easy to bring children up these days, I am told. These kids are going to turn out okay thanks to Sarah and Mike.

Mike's got a pot belly stove in his basement, which is really not a basement in the usual sense, more like the first floor of what people call a split level house. He has the stove running most of the time in the winter. Bear and I live in this room. The stove can be pretty hot, if you get too close to it. There's a TV in the room, so in the evening Mike and Sarah and the children and Bear and I get together here to watch TV. Bear and I sleep here. I really miss Heidi. I wonder how long it takes a dog to get over the loss of her best friend.

Winter, 1988

Dear Diary,

Poor Mike. Everything was going so well at the printing plant where he works when he had a freak accident. Mike is very big and strong, so you wouldn't expect him to damage his back picking up a heavy roll of paper and placing it on a press. But that is what happened. It is quite serious. He will be at home in bed for a number of weeks and then an operation. He will get disability insurance payments, but they won't cover his expenses. Sarah will probably have to go to work for a while to help make ends meet.

You know how I love to fetch tennis balls. Well, one day, when there wasn't any snow on the ground, I was having a grand time fetching. When we finished, my master forgot to take the ball from me and I went into the house and chewed on it. A piece of the ball came loose and I swallowed it. I didn't think any more about it at the time.

The next day I began to get stomach pains and then I had trouble relieving myself and I began skipping meals, which alerted my master that something was wrong. He brought me to a local vet who examined me and X-rayed my insides but couldn't find anything wrong. I got steadily worse. I couldn't eat and I got a fever. At Deb's suggestion (she's a nurse), my master took me to another vet in White Plains, who examined me and concluded I had some kind of obstruction in my intestines, which wouldn't show up on an X-ray. He operated on me and discovered the tennis ball fragment had lodged in my intestines and caused gangrene. He removed the fragment and sewed me up. When I came to, I heard him tell my master that if another day had passed, I would have been dead. That was close. Too close.

I still like to fetch tennis balls, but you can be sure I don't take them inside to chew. I learned my lesson alright. I guess that's the way you learn, by experience. Humans are better off. They learn not from experience alone but from what they are told and what they read. Except in the case of teenagers, my master insists. For them, he says, the wheel has to be re-invented and fire re-discovered by each new generation.

Dogs have a basic intelligence but we are also creatures of habit. A lot of things we learn by repetition, like getting housebroken. Oh, was that ever a dreadful experience! I was just a pup but I remember it well. I really tested the patience of my master and mistress. I was on very thin ice, but finally one day I learned. Thank God.

I am not sure how I learned to peel a banana or crack open a walnut. But I am pretty good at it. Sometimes at night I get a craving for food. I can reach up to the counter top and if there is anything edible there, I can knock it to the floor. If it is beyond my reach, Snuf will oblige. My master insists there's some kind of conspiracy between the two of us. I love bananas and walnuts. I know I will be in trouble the next day when my master or mistress discovers the litter of peels and shells on the kitchen floor, but really I can't help myself.

I have heard the expression that a particular person is "top dog." I am not exactly sure what it means. I certainly do not mind the association. If anyone wants to use me as an example of superiority, that's okay. We labs do have certain exceptional qualities. We are very, very loyal. I adore my mistress and master and will do anything for them. I think the relationship that dogs in general have with their masters is very unique. It doesn't exist among cats. They'll stay with you as long as you continue to feed them but skip a meal or two and they will start looking for another home. Of course, what I just wrote does not apply to Snuf. He's very loyal. I have heard the story that Snuf travelled fifteen miles across highly trafficked parkways in bitter winter weather to get back to Knollwood from

Ardsley, where he was temporarily boarding. It took him several days but he made it. Snuf is an exceptional cat. I believe he thinks he is a dog.

Good news about my master's book, "Tales of Bequia." It will be published in the spring. He is working very hard on the shingles book when he can find the time.

Spring, 1988.

Dear Diary,

My master and mistress sailed to Mustique one day last winter during their holiday on Bequia. I understand that Mustique is where the jet set go to get away from it all. Very posh. Very expensive. Very artificial.

My master's book on Bequia has been published. A few small publications gave it a good review, but the bigger ones like the Times just weren't interested.

My master talked to Mike about taking his children to the Bronx Zoo. I understand it is one of the best zoos in the world. There is scarcely a species that is not exhibited there in a surrounding that comes very close to its natural habitat. I would like to go with them but I guess that is not possible.

I have never been to Animal Land but I am told that there is an unusual zoo there. Perhaps somebody is pulling my leg but according to some of my acquaintances there is a zoo in Animal Land that houses a collection of humans from the far corners of the world and are shown in their natural habitat. A few examples. Homo sapiens Americanus: aggressive, carries an attache case stuffed with papers, including the Wall Street Journal, lives in cramped quarters in a tall building, eats and drinks more than he should, earns a lot of money but lives beyond his means. There is homo sapiens sporticus. He is very muscular, gets paid a lot for his athletic skills, and has a great deal of trouble with his syntax. Of course, homo sapiens politicus. Unfortunately, his brain never fully developed, which is compensated for by an unusual ability to talk but say nothing and to make unkeepable promises. He beats his breast a lot and speaks in riddles. Then there is homo sapiens performus who screeches, shouts, whines, raps, jumps about, rotates his hips, and pops his pelvis. There are many other specimens and they live in a large enclosed area that is supposed to duplicate their natural surroundings, like an office building, a football field, a rostrum, and a stage. You are not supposed to feed them when you visit, except for the special kind of food you can purchase from a vending machine. I think it is called novelle cuisine pizza and it comes in many delicious flavors and is fat free and low in cholesterol.

Summer, 1988.

Dear Diary,

So it is summer again, my favorite season. Favorite because it is so nice to lie out in the sun and bake. Dogs don't get skin cancer, so it's okay. Snuf is doing just fine for an old codger. His secret is he doesn't realize how old he really is. He's like George Burns. There's a difference. Snuf has given up on sex.

My master continues to receive literature about the abuses that animals are subjected to. The literature isn't about dogs, but I know of cases where dogs are treated pretty poorly. There's a pack of wild dogs in my neighborhood. Probably thrown out of their homes, or else they've run away to escape abuse. I have been thinking about organizing the dogs in my neighborhood to form some kind of organization, call it a commune, the purpose of which would be to protect and enhance their rights. What rights do I have in mind? The right to be treated fairly and not abused. The right of due process. In other words a dog can't be booted out of his home without reasonable cause, or denied at least one square meal a day. It seems to me that we have an unwritten contract with our owners, which provides that for the love and protection we give, we are entitled to home and board. I am not thinking of myself. I am well cared for. But there are dogs in the neighborhood that are not cared for and need protection. There's one dog who goes from house to house for food and lodging because his master just can't be bothered. I won't mention his master's name, because that would probably make matters worse.

I would not go so far as to set up a welfare state. In order to join the commune a dog must have credentials. He must be law abiding and willing to work. He must also be able to demonstrate a sense of responsibility. The commune will have laws and each member will be required to know and support them. We will have elections but the right to vote will be determined by the member's understanding and acceptance of our laws. There are a couple of rotwilers and dobermans who probably won't qualify unless they go to some sort of school and are taught how to behave properly and to conform to our constitution. Yes, I think we should have a constitution. All dogs are created equal and are entitled to life, liberty, and the pursuit of happiness. Provided, of course, they do not infringe on the freedom of other dogs. I guess you would describe my approach as qualified democracy. The right to vote does not come automatically. You earn it by virtue of your understanding and acceptance of your responsibilities as a citizen of the commune.

It's different from your approach to democracy, master. In your society everybody votes, whether qualified or not. My approach is like Plato's, which to me makes more sense. (Is it Plato or Pluto? I am not sure which.) Our society would not exclude anyone. The qualification test would be applied to all dogs and not to just the troublesome ones like rotwilers, dobermans, and pitbulls.

What do you think of my idea?

Fall, 1988.

Dear Diary,

We've elected a new president. He's quite different from his predecessor, who sat tall in the saddle. This one is more like an Arizona Road Runner. You know the bird who doesn't fly but races around the ground in circles at great speed. My master preferred the loser, a Greek, who, he thought, would be able to identify better with our domestic problems. He said he voted with the interests of his children in mind, since there wasn't much that either candidate could do to affect the rest of his life one way or the other.

My master is quite busy working on his book about shingles. He has contacted many medical research organizations around the country to get information. When he gets a return call, it is usually for Dr. Thomsen. My mistress normally responds saying that he is not a doctor. That became awkward after a while, so she doesn't bother to correct the caller anymore.

Sad news. Melanie and Pedro seem to be having their problems. My mistress says she was much too young to get married. She was just eighteen. But she could not be dissuaded. Part of the problem is that she is very headstrong and wants everything her way. She should grow out of that in time. I hope.

I had a strange dream last night. I dreamt I was visiting a place called Pitfox Land in some remote part of the world. The inhabitants were all pitfoxes and they were an aggressive lot. They had owned Pitfox Land many years ago, lost it and only recently repossessed it from neighboring razorbacks and dobermans. The razorbacks and dobermans were prepared to fight to get the land back, except for the fact that Pitfox Land had a very strong ally in the west who vowed to come to its aid in the event of an attack. It was a strange relationship between Pitfox Land and this western country called United Animals. United Animals was peopled by a diverse collection of breeds—collies, labs, terriers, golden retrievers, mastiffs, boxers, Irish wolfhounds, wimpets, just about every breed, including pitfoxes. While the population of pitfoxes was very small, it was very vocal and aggressive and did an effective job of lobbying the government so that the government pretty much did their bidding. When the pitfoxes said jump, the president (he's a wimpet) jumped and congress (mostly wimpets) also jumped, and quite high. This strange relationship went on until it became very embarrassing for the government. The last straw was when the president was requested to wear a funny little beanie that was worn by many pitfoxes. Driven by consensus, he wore it once. But that was a mistake. The response from the media was ferocious. That started a national reaction. The animals in United Animals got together, marched on the capital, and demanded an end to the relationship. The pitfoxes growled but they were outnumbered. The president met them in the petunia garden, waved to the TV cameras, and struck a deal. It was quite a deal. Those pitfoxes who wanted to emigrate to Pitfox Land would have their passage paid and receive an affirmative, head-start contribution of twenty five thousand dollars. Those who opted to stay would find their lobbying activities restricted by a users tax. Labor unions, manufacturers, and other special interests were not enthusiastic about the tax that would affect their lobbying activities too, but they were persuaded that it was a small price to pay. When the president made the announcement, he fidgeted nervously (a typical wimpet response), waved again to the cameras, and proclaimed that a thousand points of light had been preserved.

Winter, 1989.

Dear Diary,

I am back at our house on Adams Farm. When my master and mistress go away on winter vacation, I visit with Mike and Sarah and their children and Bear at their home in New Fairfield. Chelsea is going to be five in a few months and will start kindergarten. Jordan is just two. They now have two dogs, Dutchess and Bear. Dutchess is a chocolate lab, which Deb gave them as a present. She's very active and high strung, which is unusual for a lab. She is having the same housebreaking problem that I had when I was a pup.

It's good to be home. I missed Snuf, who stayed at Debs. He's a character. He licked my face again. I don't know what's with him. Cats aren't supposed to do that.

I have written before about Animal Land. You know I am not sure it really exists. Some of my canine friends swear that they have friends who have friends who have been to Animal Land. Maybe it exists only in my dreams.

From what I hear, Animal Land must be like what humans call Shangri-la. Most animals live in peace with one another. There are no predators, or predatorees. (Is there such a word?) They are healthy and free. They don't need laws to protect them from one another. They live together in what seems to be perfect harmony. They have respect for one another and it doesn't matter what breed they are, or their color, or their configuration.

Animal Land must be a wonderful place and I wish I knew how to get there. I wouldn't stay. Just visit. I have a pretty good deal here and I wouldn't trade it for anything. Maybe it doesn't exist for mortals. Maybe it is like what humans call heaven. Maybe I will get there when the time comes to depart this world. Maybe I will get there sooner than I realize. That's a dumb thought. I am like my master who expects to live on forever.

Ever so often I get the urge to roam. There are some dogs in the neighborhood who are free to wander. When my master takes me out for a walk, I see them running in the open fields, or down at the creek, or coming out of the woods. They look excited and very happy. I would like to run with them. At least once. It must be a wonderful feeling to run free, completely, absolutely free.

Spring, 1989

Dear Diary,

Winter is over and spring is at hand. Winter is officially over when people take down their deer fences. Deer were a problem again this past winter. They were all over the area scavenging for food. If you don't protect your plantings with deer fencing, you won't have them by winter's end. I would like to run with them. But they are too fast for me.

I saw my first dead deer. My master took me along with him for a ride when he went shopping. The deer lay alongside Route 55, hit by a car. I felt very sorry for the deer. His life was over. If only he had realized the danger he was in trying to cross a busy road. Deer don't seem to have any sense of fear. They certainly do not fear humans. They are all over the neighborhood. They graze as if the place belonged to them. I guess it once did before the houses were built. Sometimes very early in the morning just before daybreak I hear the wailing of dogs. My master thinks they are coyotes. He's not sure whether they migrated here from the Adirondacks, or were brought in to keep the deer from taking over. I find the idea of importing coyotes to kill deer repulsive. My master says a better way of controlling the deer population would be to sterilize a certain number. He says that could be done by adding certain chemicals to their food. That would seem to be a humane approach. Better than shooting them, as some have suggested.

If nature has its way, many will be wiped out by starvation and disease. Nature can be very cruel.

I don't understand what people see in golf. When you are through with your game, you are back where you started and five hours of precious time have been lost chasing a ball around the countryside. I got out on the course a couple of times when we lived next to the country club. I remember one time a golf ball whizzed by me and I did what my instincts instructed me to do, and that was to retrieve the ball. The golfer was very unhappy with me.

What I like most about golf and other sports are the colorful outfits that people wear. I guess people are like peacocks. Some of their outfits are pretty imaginative. Particularly the bike riders. You wouldn't think there was much sport involved in riding a bike, but boy do they get dressed up. I think they are consenting adults to the advertising hype of the garment industry.

Busy as my master is, he has still found the time to extend the deck in the back of the house. He's thinking about putting in a pool. My mistress' doctor thinks a pool is a good idea. For her. Definitely not for me.

I had hoped that Melanie and Pedro would be able to patch up their differences She is very critical of him and he thinks everything is a joke.

Late spring, 1989

Dear Diary,

I'm not watching as much TV as I used to. Neither is my master or mistress. They had cable put in. It lasted about two months, then they had it removed. Just more junk.

My mistress prefers to read and my master to write. Snuf and I are getting more sleep. I guess we are beginning to show our age. Snuf must be an old fellow. He belonged to Melanie when she was just a child. My mistress says I am graying around the muzzle.

I am unhappy about the way our system of government is functioning. We are not handling our domestic problems very well. There are too many homeless, and many are homeless for no other reason than that the cost of living has advanced faster than their income, and maybe that's because so many better paying jobs have been exported to other countries. I wonder if our Congressmen are really in tune with the times. To me they seem remote. I can't see my Congressman fixing the plumbing when there is a leak, or changing a diaper, or fixing the flat on his car, or shopping at the supermarket, or walking the streets of any large city, or paying the bills at the end of the month. They seem more concerned with doing what is required to return them to office at election time. That means doing favors for their more important constituents, so that they will cough up funds to finance their reelection. It's kind of a game that you can't lose, unless you do something very stupid.

I am bothered too by the many who take advantage of their office and abuse their privileges and perks. I think we should set up an office in government to single out, identify, and publicize the offenders. A good name for such an office would be the Office of Public Offenders. I like the ring of that. We have an Office of Public Defenders. Why not Public Offenders?

I wish I could do something about it. Maybe I could collect signatures from dogs in the neighborhood and send a petition to Millie in the White House. Do you suppose anything would come of it?

Summer, 1989.
Dear Diary,
We now have a swimming pool in our backyard. It was built very quickly, in less than a month. It fits in perfectly. I am tempted to go in. It looks inviting, particularly on a hot day. But let's face it. I am afraid of water.

My master and mistress look different and funny when they are in the pool, with only their heads showing and I am standing above them looking down at them. For a brief moment I feel superior. It looks like fun paddling around in the water but I am satisfied to watch them having fun. I keep my distance even when the pool is covered at night. You would think that I might forget and try walking on the cover. Never. I am smarter than that. I instinctively know what would happen. I am not so smart that I have figured out a new contraption that the boss has bought and put in the pool. He calls it Creepy Charlie. It scoots around the bottom of the pool collecting dirt. It even climbs the walls. When I first saw it, I thought it was coming out of the pool after me, so I barked and got into a crouch, prepared to attack when it climbed out of the pool. It stopped just short of getting out and then wisely backed off. I guess I frightened it off. Sometimes we are nose to nose. But I stand my ground and in time he retreats. I know now that it won't or can't get out of the pool, so I have learned to accept Creepy Charlie. I guess there is some kind of lesson in that. Like standing your ground, knowing that in time things will work out your way.

Sometimes that philosophy just doesn't work. I am thinking of Melanie and Pedro. They have decided to separate and he has gone back to Portugal. Melanie is upset. She knows she is partly to blame but she is stubborn. I hope they get together somehow.

I understand that they have started something new in Animal Land called the Academy Rewards. I guess it is supposed to be some kind of spoof. Noteworthy people are named for these rewards and later busts commemorating the winners are installed in a museum for animals to visit and see. I think it is a cross between the competitions we have here for outstanding actors, actresses, and directors, to cite a few that come to mind, and the hall of fame museums for athletes. The rewards are given to people, not animals. That's a twist. You would think that in Animal Land animals would compete for the rewards. You'll get the drift when I mention some of the people who have been nominated. Here's a partial list. President Bush for his ability to talk out of both sides of his mouth, which won him the cover of Time Magazine. Ted Kennedy for his outstanding performance in "American Tragedy." Ronald Reagan for best actor ever in the White House. David Dinkins for his delicate performance in "Tight Rope." Gerald Ford for golf pro of the year. Mikel Gorbachev for best international straddle. Saddam Husein for his role in "Deception." Sununu for his performance in "Above and Beyond." Madam Ambassador to Iraq, April Glaspie, for her nimble performance in "Cat on a Hot Tin Roof." Governor Cuomo for his rendition of "Bewitched, Bothered and Bewildered." Jesse Jackson for playing the lead in the highly successful west coast rock group, "Niggers with Attitudes." Sharfton tried to join the group but was nosed out by Jackson.

I am a little surprised by the last nomination. Sounds a little below the belt. On the other hand, maybe they deserve it. It will be interesting to see how the competitions develop and who the winners are.

Fall, 1989.

Dear Diary,

One thing that Melanie has and that is chutzbah. She left for Portugal a few weeks ago to try to patch things up with Pedro. She returned a few days ago and I heard her talking with my master. Apparently, she had a great time. She stayed with Pedro at a cottage on the Algarve. It was a second honeymoon. They had their vows renewed at a local church. Pedro's dad was enthusiastic. His mother was not. She wants Pedro to stay in Portugal and has tried hard to make it attractive to him. Melanie says that Pedro plans to return to the States right after Christmas and before New Years. I certainly hope so. He seems to be quite important to her. I don't know what she sees in him, but my opinions on such a matter don't count.

Mike is happy in his new job at the printing company. He is working in the sample department. It's quite different from the job he had as a pressman, which he can't handle anymore because of his damaged back.

My master still calls Mike a kid, although he is over thirty. There's been quite a change in Mike. As a kid he was kind of wild, my master says. He is very much a family man now. His main sources of entertainment are his family, fishing and hunting. He's very good at all.

Debbie has accumulated a bunch of cats. It's her family, she says. Which I think is kind of sad. She loves children. She has Melanie but she should have many more. I've met a couple of her cats and they're okay but nothing like Snuf. I think Snuf is one-of-a-kind cat.

Snuf just gave me a lick to get my attention. He gets kind of annoyed when I spend a lot of time writing. He craves attention. He caught me on the nose with his paw a few days ago. Fortunately, his claws were not extended. I was quite surprised. Then he rubbed the side of his face against mine and purred and I knew he was telling me he was sorry. I don't think there's another cat in the world like Snuf.

Late fall, 1989.
Dear Diary,
I am concerned about animal rights and I have been thinking about trying to elicit Millie's support in the White House. I suppose Millie is quite busy being photographed with the rich and famous who visit the President but if she's the caring kind of dog that I think she is, I am sure she can break away and find the time to give us her support. I think her support could make a big difference in trying to arouse the public. I think I will write her a letter and this is what I intend to say.

"Dear Millie, I am writing you this letter because I am sure you feel, as I do, that the rights of animals are constantly being abused and will continue to be abused until the public becomes concerned and involved. I am sure you have seen the dreadful photographs of calves and chickens being warehoused in dreadful conditions, awaiting the time when they will be killed to put meat on the table, and that you feel as I do that these atrocities must be brought to an end.

"Let me get to the point. I am hopeful that you can be persuaded to alert our President to the dreadful things that are going on in the meat packing industry. We are endeavoring to start a bandwagon of outraged citizens and we hope that the President can be prevailed upon to join the bandwagon, if not lead it. You know better than I how good he is at climbing on bandwagons, particularly when there are TV cameras around, and I feel certain this will appeal to him as a true animal lover. If you have the opportunity to discuss this with him, as I am sure you will, please be sure that he does not seek the counsel of the Inner Circle, who, I am sure, would resist any effort to place limits of any kind on the spirit of free enterprise as practiced by the meat packing industry. If you think it would help, I think I could persuade Lassie, Dinah, Asta, Smokie and other notables to join a delegation of concerned animals to pay a visit to you and your master. I can visualize a splendid picture opportunity that should appeal to the President. There he is sitting on the floor of his Oval Office surrounded by adoring dogs. I can anticipate one danger that we must be alert to and that is the possibility of a liberal newspaper captioning the photograph, "President Goes to the Dogs." I think we can pre-empt that possibility by getting the President to announce to the cameras in advance that he wants to become known as the Animal-Lover President. Considering the difficulties he has had promoting himself as the Education President, he will probably welcome the opportunity to shift focus. It would be quite a coup if he disclosed that he has resisted veal, like brocoli, since his mother tried to force it on him when he was very young. I am sure you have a lot of thoughts, Millie, on how we could mount a campaign against the butchering of animals. Hope to hear from you soon.

Early winter, 1989

Dear Diary,

I look forward to Sundays. It has become a time when members of the family come together. Not every Sunday because then it would become a routine. But often enough so that it has a place in the course of events that I can look forward to. Mike and Sarah bring their children, Chelsea and Jordan. Deb will come if she is not stuck with extra duty as a nurse and Melanie is what I would call an irregular regular. In the summer there is a lot of activity revolving around the pool. At this time of the year the focus of attention swings between the fireplace in the living room and the TV room. I love a fire in the fireplace. Mike will sprawl on the floor in front of it. So will I. My master will read the Sunday Times. The children like to bang away at the piano. My mistress tries to show them the correct way of fingering the piano keys. They have a good time learning to play and when they are finished my mistress will play for them and the family. I am more than a little envious. I wish I could learn. But that is impossible. Even I, a lab, have limitations. That's a fact.

My mistress usually goes to church on Sundays before the family assembles. My master joins her on important occasions like Christmas and Easter. He says that he doesn't have to go along the rest of the time because she punches his ticket for him. I think I understand why people go to church. Believing in another world is a very important and necessary anchor for most people, and church is a pleasant and moving way of expressing that belief. We dogs don't have a church to go to and our beliefs are different. I believe in the goodness of my master and mistress and I think there is a place that I will go to when my time is up and that is Animal Land. There things are good and peaceful and there is godliness in everything. My master says I am a pantheist. I think he is too.

My master usually has some chores to perform when my mistress is at church. Like getting ready to serve something special for breakfast when she returns. He's good at soufflés. Under the circumstances she doesn't fuss too much when he remains at home. I love soufflés. I love most anything that is edible and there are darn few things that are not edible.

Dumbo Land goes through crazes just as we do here. I understand there is a new rock group in Dumbo Land called Dobermans With Attitudes. Their lyrics are pretty nasty. A similar group tried to get started in Animal Land but the other animals strongly objected and pressured the owl, who runs things in Animal Land, to do something about it. The owl consulted with his council and then took firm, decisive action. The rock group was deported to Dumbo Land, where they had originally come from. Some of the civil rights groups objected, but they were reminded that freedom of speech is not an absolute right and that it has limitations. The owl said it cannot be construed to permit obscenity. It seems to me that the owl is a pretty savvy guy. I wonder if he could be cloned. We sure could use someone like him to help run things here.

Winter, 1990.

Dear Diary,

It was a happy Christmas for most members of the family but not for Melanie. She learned a few days earlier that Pedro, who had promised to return, had decided to stay in Portugal. His mother made it almost impossible for him to leave. She gave him a house and a car and got him involved in her department store. Melanie was crushed. She thought they had patched matters up but apparently not.

Would you believe it? I am eight. I am catching up with my master and mistress who are also senior citizens. They don't act like they are senior citizens and sometimes must give proof when they go to the movies and ask for a senior's discount. I like my naps which are more frequent now. I still like to run but I get tired more quickly.

My master has a fire going in the fireplace, which is very nice on a cold day like this. I like to curl up in front of a fire and reminisce. Dogs do that, you know. We've got memories, good ones and bad. All of mine have been good. Well, most of them. I still remember getting spanked with paper when I was a pup and wet where I shouldn't have, and the time my master thought he could teach me to swim by tossing me in the lake. I like to remember Heidi who was so majestic and friendly and the silly doves and the awful skunk who did a number on me and my friend the fox from Animal Land and the many, many animals who came around our house on the pond. I remember all the wonderful experiences I had as a pup and how thoughtful and loving my master and mistress have been. I guess that's enough nostalgia for the moment.

My master read in the paper that Memphis, Tennessee, is building a pyramid to help identify it with Egypt and to attract tourists. It seems more than a little far out to me. Next you will read that the citizens of Paris, Texas, are going to construct a replica of the Eifel Tower. You can take this pretty far. Humans are strange at times. Corny is a better word.

We had a cocktail party a few days ago and there was a lot of talk about political correctness. As I understand it, what this means is that people should be very polite in their dealings with minorities and not use offensive language. There's strong opposition to the idea. Many say that it infringes on the principle of freedom of speech. I like the idea of good manners but I don't think it can or should be stuffed down one's throat. It is something that you acquire as you mature and learn to deal with people. Any lab, properly brought up, knows that.

Freedom of speech is still more important than good manners. It is a right while manners are something you may or may not come by. I think that if the ones who are taunted would do a little more to earn respect, the situation would change and the problem of correctness would disappear. At least that's a lab's perspective. How do you see it Millie from the White House?

Late winter, 1990

Dear Diary,

One of the funniest sights I have ever seen is my master exercising on his rowing machine. He got the machine as a gift from his son, when Mike couldn't use it any longer because of his bad back. Exercising is one of the first routines on his schedule after breakfast. He moves forth and back on the machine like he is rowing a boat. I remember the first time I saw him on the machine. I came up real close and flopped on the floor in front of him. I crossed my paws and cradled my head on my paws and just watched in amazement. I must have had a funny look on my face because my master laughed. Jokingly he invited me to get into the machine with him, which, of course, I declined. There are times when he underestimates my intelligence. No way would I try to get into what seems to me to be a useless machine.

My master rows endlessly, it seems, but he doesn't get anywhere. I think the expression 'a long run for a short slide' applies. So what's the point. He rows for quite a while and when he's finished, he struggles to get out of the contraption and he is breathing heavily, so much so that I worry about him. That kind of exercise looks like work. I think he would be better off if he learned to run and fetch like me. Now that's exercise and also fun.

Spring, 1990

Dear Diary,

My master's book on shingles has been published. I saw a copy of it on the cocktail table in the living room. I think my master's preoccupation with writing the book helped him deal with the pain he was suffering. He is looking a lot better these days.

I understand he is at work now on a novel. Actually, he's been at it for several years. He showed a draft to an agent who said it was too flat. Darling Melanie, who was eighteen at the time, said she could fix that up. Wouldn't surprise me a bit, if she could.

Melanie's got a job in the travel field, which she likes very much. It helps her take her mind off her problems with Pedro. She is hurt and angry and has decided to initiate divorce proceedings, which won't be easy since he has no intention of leaving Portugal.

I have been hearing about the epidemic of AIDS, which has got a lot of people upset. It seems to me that there has been too much hype by the media. The people mostly at risk are the homosexuals and the drug addicts and they account for a very small percentage of the population, thank God.

Since I turned eight, age has been on my mind. I don't feel that I am getting older, except that I like to nap more often. But perhaps I didn't nap enough before and now I am just catching up. For a dog, age does not creep up on you. It happens all at once. One day you are a pup and the next day you are a senior.

I had another visit from J. Sylvan Fox. It was nice to see him again. His last visit was quite a while ago. He brought along an associate of his from Dumbo Land. I should say his associate had come from Dumbo Land originally. He has applied for entrance to Animal Land as a refugee and has been accepted. He's a squirrel and he looks a little strange—kind of shabby looking like he's been through a wringer. I guess you get to look that way when you spend any amount of time on Dumbo Land. Apparently, he was well educated, because when he graduated from business school, he easily got a good paying job on Bawl Street in the bond department of Salmon Brothers. He says he burned out in just a few years and wished he hadn't gotten into finance. He has already found a good job in Animal Land working for a manufacturer, where his skills and knowledge as a business school graduate are most valuable. He says that's the direction he should have taken when he got out of school. But like most other graduates he was attracted by the big bucks that are paid on Bawl Street.

Sylva said the economy in Dumbo Land is in pretty bad shape, partly because of scandals in the finance and banking industries. He said there is a moral sickness in the land. It stems from a culture that emphasizes "me," "money," "power," and "greed." The media has labelled the new upward, mobile generation as "Gimmees," which stands for "greed is me." Apparently, the label is appropriate and acceptable because none of the new breed seems offended.

Every year people on Bawl Street publish a satire on the workings of the "street" and call it the Bawl Street Journal. They ridicule and lampoon the firms they work for and the ways their companies are run. Sylva says it is a form of catharsis, an expiation for misdeeds and misconduct. He says that each year, on the Day of Atonement, places of worship are very well attended. Confession is also very popular, so popular it cannot be conducted on a one-to-one basis in a confessional booth any longer, but requires a large open area like a stadium. Participants announce at the beginning of their confession that they are money addicts and need forgiveness.

"So far this new culture hasn't arrived in Animal Land," Sylva said, "but it could happen. A land like ours, which is free and idealistic, is always vulnerable."

On that note he and his friend, the squirrel, left. I had meant to ask Sylva how one got to Animal Land but he got away before I could ask.

Summer, 1990

Dear Diary,

We have a new member of our family, Dutchess, a chocolate lab. Mike was having problems training her and was about ready to throw in the towel, when my master said he would like to have the dog as company for me. She has been with us now for a while and apparently isn't a problem. She's kind of high strung, which is unusual for a lab. She can run much faster than I and faster than any other dog around here. She's also a good watch dog, which frankly I am not. She can hear people approaching the house when they are quite a distance away and can she bark!

She's great company. We sleep together, eat together, run together. I should include Snuf, who doesn't know he is a cat. I was surprised how easily Dutchess and Snuf got along from the very start. Its a regular kibutz, the three of us. Like old times when Heidi was alive.

At first we slept in the kitchen on two overstuffed cushions. We were moved to the laundry room when I learned how to open the counter cupboards and help myself to whatever I could find that was edible. Snuf is part of the conspiracy. He can open doors that I can't and his ability to jump comes in handy when there is something delicious on the counter that I can't reach. Dutchess doesn't get involved. She's more circumspect. That's interesting.

I really don't like being confined. There's a sliding pocket door between the kitchen and the dining room, which I learned to open with my nose and paws. Now, when we are left alone, my master will place a kitchen chair against the door to keep me from opening it. One day I will figure out a way to move the chair. Yes, I can be mischievous, but not in a really mischievous way. It's kind of a game I play. I don't get spanked anymore, haven't been since I was a pup. I suppose I would behave better if I thought I might get spanked. The worst that happens to me is a scolding. I respond with my baby-eyed expression. He laughs and that's that.

My master's book on shingles is selling quite well. The first printing sold out in two months and Cross River Press has ordered a second printing.

My master and mistress are enjoying their pool. Dutchess and Snuf have the same aversion to water that I have. We are content to sit on the deck and observe. I am getting used to Creepy Charlie and I was surprised that Dutchess wasn't at all fazed. Took the little monster right in stride. Snuf is still hunting chipmunks. But since he is belled, he isn't very successful. He is doing a lot more napping, which is to be expected considering his age. So am I.

Fall, 1990.

Dear Diary,

I still love to fetch. Everyday Dutchess and I get a chance to fetch. My master has damaged his right shoulder, so he has learned to throw a tennis ball with his left arm and he's getting better at it all the time. I am not as agile as I used to be and Dutchess is faster at retrieving than I am. Ever so often my master tries to trick Dutchess. He feints a forward throw and when Dutchess starts to run, he flips it backward so that I have a better chance at retrieving the ball. I can usually get there first and make the retrieve. I make believe that I am not aware of my master's little deception and honestly I do not think that Dutchess knows what is going on. Anyway I feel good about it, and so does Dutchess, who makes more retrieves than I, and my master feels good too. I suppose it is necessary to play these little games, call them deceits, from time to time to keep things in balance.

We had quite an adventure the other day. My master took us out for our morning walk, when Dutchess spotted a deer and took off, and I followed, trying to keep up. We were deep in the woods and I was lost. I didn't know where I was and how to get back. I had not had any breakfast, so I was quite hungry. I wandered around for hours and was getting quite tired. I sloshed around in a swamp and got pretty dirty. It was late in the day when I finally emerged from the woods and found myself on a main and busy road. I crossed the road and it's a wonder I did not get hit by a car. A very nice lady stopped. She knew I was lost. She called to me and of course, being a lab, I came. She checked my dog tag and found my name and address. An attendant at a local gas station told her how to get to my house. She brought me there and rang the bell. I remember my master's and mistress' response when they opened the door. They were speechless for a moment and then overcome with excitement and relief. I learned later that they had spent most of the day looking for me.

They thanked the woman profusely and offered a reward, which she refused. I learned later that what she did was most unusual. My master and mistress are still talking about it.

Dutchess was there to welcome me home. Where had she been? I found out later that she had returned in the morning with a boy friend, a big German shepherd, and they proceeded to have an affair right on the front lawn. My master was away looking for me and my mistress was afraid to break it up. When he returned, he called the vet and was told to bring Dutchess in, which he did the next day. I understand that Dutchess will not have a litter now or ever. At least she had one fling, which is more than I had. I am not sure you know that dogs can smile. If you look closely, you will see one on Dutchess' face. Fairly big. But none on mine.

Late fall, 1990.
Dear Diary,
There seems to be trouble brewing in Dumbo Land. It never was a place that I wanted to visit. Now it is becoming downright unpleasant, so I am told. Permissive is the word. Obscenity seems to be in. In art galleries, movies, TV, newspapers. It is protected by a weird interpretation of freedom of speech.

My neighbor's dog, who has been there, says permissiveness is everywhere. In the streets particularly. One breed is causing a great deal of trouble and that is the pitbull. Pitbulls comprise what appears to be an underclass of animals that defy the law and choose to take matters into their own hands. They are concentrated in the inner cities and operate as gangs. There is violence in the streets, in movie houses, in places of worship. The gangs are vicious. They fight among themselves and killings are an everyday occurrence. The situation has truly gotten out of hand.

How has this come about? Boss (that's my neighbor's dog) says that law and order is a joke. The public seems to be afraid to take any action to control the situation. There is a bunch of politicians, who call themselves liberals, who look the other way because a vote is a vote even when it is cast by a pitbull, and they are aided and abetted by the media, for whom a story is a story is a story. I don't think there is any evil genius behind the disintegration of Dumbo Land. My guess is that the movers and shakers are a collection of discontents, malcontents, leftover radicals from the sixties, and newcomers and outcasts who aren't prepared to belong but want the structure of society changed to suit them.

I am concerned and frightened. I really don't care much about Dumbo Land but the disintegration there is beginning to take root here, in our own country, my master says. Something has to be done about it before it goes any farther. Obviously, the offenders need to be retrofitted, if that word can be applied to people. I understand that the military has closed a number of camps. Why couldn't the camps be used for this purpose? My master says the government had camps in the Great Depression, which were part of the Civilian Conservation Corps, and were designed to provide work and teach new skills. I think they are needed now more than ever.

I think I will write a letter to the Editor of the New York Times. On second thought that may not be the right publication to write to. I'm not sure how sympathetic the newspaper would be. It is a hard publication to figure out. Sometimes its editorial stance is right on the button. Sometimes it is way off. There's nothing wrong about being liberal, as long as you are sincere and forthright and motivated by concern for the common good and not by some hidden agenda. Maybe the Times would like me to write an editorial for their op-ed page. All kinds of opinion appear there. Even Safire is a regular contributor.

Early winter, 1991

Dear Diary,

I love the winter. I have written that before. So does Dutchess. Snuf wants no part of it. He absolutely refuses to come out when there is snow on the ground. Dutchess and I race around in the banks of snow to see who can kick up the most snow and emerge looking like snow men (snow dogs?).

Unfortunately, I can't run as fast or as long as I used to. I get out of breath. I think my master has noticed. He has cut down on the running and fetching and frankly I really don't mind. I think we have a pretty good understanding, my master and I. Fortunately, he doesn't have to prove himself by running. But he's got his own challenges. For a retired person, he is very busy. Sometimes he doesn't have the time to take me out and then it is up to my mistress to walk me, which I like because she doesn't walk as fast and never runs.

I am reminded from time to time that I am not getting any younger. I don't like to think about getting old. For dogs there isn't any place of last resort, like a nursing home. I would like to hang around for a very long time and I know my master and mistress share this feeling.

Leaving this earth, which will happen one day, is a stinking idea. We were placed her for a reason and surely that reason was not to die. There really must be something more. Maybe I am a coward and looking for an anchor to hang on to, because I am afraid. Humans and animals, we are all so frail and vulnerable. Our only defense is our faith. It may come to you as a surprise, but we animals also believe.

We don't have a formal religion like humans. Maybe that's fortunate. You humans have so many religions and in many important ways they are identical, and yet wars have been fought in their names. Isn't that ridiculous? All of us seem to need the strength of purpose that comes with faith and yet we question its authenticity when it does not exactly match ours. Maybe we're not so bright afterall. You notice I am lumping us together, humans and animals.

New Years Day, 1991.

Dear Diary,

I understand that this is a day when people make resolutions. I suppose I should, too. I wish for a perfect world and that I can be part of it. It is a dream, isn't it? I heard my master talk about the prophet Isaias and his prediction of the coming of Christ. I heard him quote from the Old Testament, "The wolf shall dwell with the lamb; and the leopard shall lie down with the kid; and the calf and the lion and sheep shall abide together, and a little child shall lead them." As I listened, I thought of Animal Land. I believe that is the way it is in Animal Land. All of the animals live together in peace and harmony. The more I think about it, the more certain I become that Animal Land is real, that it exists not just in my dreams but in my expectations. I think it is a goal, something to be achieved, hopefully in this lifetime, but, if not, then in what may lie ahead. The little child is a metaphor for goodness, simplicity, honesty, trust. Now, I will make my New Year's resolution, that I can become like the little child and lead my brethren.

Winter, 1991

Dear Diary,

My master says his timing is magical. The war with Iraq started the day they left for Bequia and it ended the day they returned. They didn't get much news about the war's progress while they were away, and so were a little surprised by the degree to which people were preoccupied with the war when they returned. It was a strange war. It seemed almost tailor-made for our president to refute the allegation of being a wimp. That's my master's point of view. It's hard to believe that this war could not have been averted. I don't know how. War is madness. Even in Dumbo Land animals are smart enough to keep disputes from getting out of hand. I understand there are going to be many parades when our soldiers return and I like the idea of the yellow ribbons. I hope our sense of patriotism doesn't get out of hand and turn into a farce. The way it unfolds will depend a lot on the way it is hyped by politicians and the media. Sometimes I think people are like puppets and can be jerked around and manipulated at will.

Late winter, 1991

Dear Diary,

There's a very nice dog in the neighborhood called Rusty who isn't appreciated by his owners. He's a mixed breed, with long gray-black hair, and about medium size. He has a home but prefers to live anywhere else. He stays with various families in the area and takes his meals where he can get them. He's not abused in the usual sense. Just not loved.

He visits with me from time to time. I am glad to share what I have with him and sometimes he stays over. Until yesterday I hadn't seen him in at least a month and I was getting worried. When he showed up, he told me he had taken a long trip to Animal Land and also Dumbo Land. I asked him how he had gotten there, since I would like to visit Animal Land someday. He said he was transported. I didn't understand, so he explained that he started in a northerly direction and in the evening found a cave where he fell asleep. When he awakened, he found himself in a new and strange land. Everything was quite beautiful and the animals he met were very friendly. He asked where he was and he was told he was in Animal Land.

"I made a lot of friends and they put me up and gave me food and, most important, love," he said. "My new friends told me about Dumbo Land, which intrigued me, because it sounded so screwed up, so I decided to pay a visit. They told me to get back as soon as possible because it wasn't the kind of place where you would want to stay.

"It was quite an experience," Rusty said, "and I am sorry I went. It's hard to describe. A great deal of poverty, violence in the streets, crime—a very unpleasant place.

"People in jail were better off. They got three squares a day, a roof over their heads and they were safer than animals on the outside. Getting into jail became quite popular. Some animals committed minor crimes just for the chance to get into jail. There were even lotteries with prizes ranging from one to ten years. As you might imagine, even the most honest animals began cheating on their income taxes in the hope they would be caught and sent to jail."

"Soon the jails were overcrowded and now the government had a problem of trying to discourage crime. The president of Dumbo Land came up with an ingenious solution. He arranged to have TV sets installed in every cell and to be run continuously day in and day out. Well, you know how bad TV programming has become in our country, with sit-coms on every channel. In Dumbo Land programming has become even worse. News programs, dramas, sports are gone and in their place sit-coms all day and all night. As you might guess, even the most hardened criminals could not tolerate sit-coms as a forced diet, without any let up. The effect was universal: inevitably your mind would become scrambled and you would begin to talk gibberish just like a politician. It looked as though the criminal population would decline as a result, until some smart medical researcher with a pharmaceutical company came up with a pill that would allow you to watch a full day of sit-coms without adverse effects. Unfortunately for the public in general and those in jail the pill had one bad side effect. If you overdosed, you developed a severe case of radio euphoria which manisfested itself in an unsatiable craving for repeats of old Jack Benny and Amos and Andy radio programs from the 20s and 30s."

I asked Rusty how the problem got resolved.

"I really don't know. I had enough of Dumbo Land and returned to Animal Land. My friends weren't surprised by my experience. They saw that I was visibly shaken and told me to get a good night's sleep and I would feel better in the morning. When I woke up, I found myself back in the cave closeby. They must have driven me back during the night. I was so tired I could have slept through an earthquake."

I was convinced more than ever that I did not want to visit Dumbo Land, whose problems were like ours but worse.

Early spring, 1991.

Dear Diary,

Dutchess and I spent February with Mike and his family when my master and mistress were away on a winter vacation. We had a great time with Bear and the children. The kids are growing up, which reminds me I turned nine. I seem a little preoccupied with age. Scarey.

When we came home, my master noticed some lumps on my chest and hind quarters. He brought me to the vet, who took a biopsy and said I had cancer. I don't know much about cancer, other than my master had it and has managed to handle it. A few days later I returned to the animal hospital and began chemotherapy. They administered a drug into one of my arteries so slowly that it took most of the day. It didn't hurt and I didn't feel any different afterwards. There were no side effects and I did not lose any hair.

I am also taking a drug which I heard my master call prednisone. I don't like the drug. It makes me hungry and thirsty and causes me to breathe faster and deeper. I am always out of breath and I can feel my heart pounding. I take it morning and night. My mistress gives it to me. She opens my mouth, gently places the pills down my throat, and strokes my neck to induce me to swallow. As a reward, I get a dog biscuit afterwards. Dutchess also gets one. The routine has become a habit. We know approximately when I am to get my pills and we line up together.

Snuf was away at Melanie's, when Dutch and I were at Mike's, and he came home with a cold that developed into pneumonia. He looked terrible and wouldn't eat. He was put on an antibiotic and in about two weeks he was back to normal.

Melanie has her own apartment, which she likes very much. She likes to be independent and tries to be. She had to be, I guess, growing up with no father on the premises and a mother who had to work. My master tried his best to be a surrogate but it didn't work so well. Melanie's got a job with a travel company. It is run by a group of Jewish women. They refer to Melanie as goy-girl. I think that is kind of funny. The problem is that without wheels she has to take a bus and a train to get to work. It takes her an hour and a half to travel a distance of just eight miles. She hopes to get her wheels soon.

I am told there is a recession going on and that a lot of people are suffering. Deb was laid off from her job as admissions director at a nursing home, but found another job fairly quickly. Mike's printing company has laid off many employees, but so far he hasn't been affected. I think it is wrong that people should suffer for something they had no role in creating and the safety net that politicians and businessmen talk about has too many holes in it to work. It seems to me that the mechanisms of our system have not kept pace with the times and badly need overhauling. I don't know the answer. I wish I did.

Spring, 1991

Dear Diary,

We have been having family get-togethers on Sundays fairly regularly in recent months. My boss is the instigator. He is like an Italian Don. A regular paters familias.

Last Sunday Deb noticed that I had developed two more growths on my backside and strongly suggested another visit to the vet. My master was surprised that he had not noticed them. The next day we went back to the vet and he suggested moving up the next chemo treatment, so my master left me with him for the day. The chemo went the same as the others. Smoothly and no side-effects. Despite this nasty infection, I feel pretty good but I don't have the spunk I had before.

The vet said that I should be walked but no strenuous exercise. I would like to fetch but I tire quickly. I think the prednisone is responsible. Dutch and I are not taken out together anymore out of deference, I guess, to my health. At least she has a chance to run and, oh, how I wish I could run with her.

Actually, I really don't mind skipping the daily run. That's what I tell myself. I don't seem to have much pep and my heart is racing all the time and I know my master is worried about that and my heavy breathing. I will find a nice comfy spot in the TV room where the sun slants through the window in the afternoon and have a siesta. No one watches TV in the afternoon, so it will be quiet. I am sure Dutchess and Snuf will join me. Snuf is an ageless wonder. Despite being belled, he caught a mouse this morning in the garden. He knows he can't bring it into the house, so he was quite content to leave it at the doorstep. My mistress gave him a pat on the head and he purred. I can still hear him purring. I wonder how he does it.

Melanie has finally gotten her wheels. It was quite an involved transaction. Mike got my master's Renault. Melanie got Mike's Toyota. And the master bought a new car, a very sporty, white Mazda. My mistress has already layed claim to the new car. She has a good argument. She is not about to relearn driving a stick-shift car, which means that my master will be driving the Protege. Melanie is in heaven. While she has driven other family cars, this is the first one that is really hers. Having her own car will make getting to and from work a lot easier.

My master seems to dote on this girl. It really isn't surprising. I understand that she spent a lot of time with them in her growing up years. Some of his friends think he is doing too much for her. I have heard her express the same thought. She wants to be independent. My master hopes the time will come when she can be independent. In the meantime, he is there for her.

I had another visit from Rusty. I recently wrote that Rusty, a neighborhood dog, had been to Animal Land and Dumbo Land and had reported on his experiences there. He said he had forgotten to tell me about the state of education in Dumbo Land, which he described as weird. He told me that conventional courses at schools had been replaced by a new kind of curriculum which he thought was quite far out. He mentioned, for example, that at Sweatmore students could enroll in a history course that "examines life and death, vocation and avocation, life after death, and the resurgency of the occult in United States popular culture." He also cited some examples of papers that had been delivered by faculty members of the Modern Language Association, which is run primarily by hyenas. He remembered the titles, "Sherlock Holmes as a Pervert," "Strategies for Teaching a Feminist Latin American Culture Course in Antartica," "Gender and Sexual Relationships in Paradise Lost," and "Sexuality in the Female Dominant Bee Hive." He said he thought the main movers behind the new thinking on educational campuses were the aging radicals of the sixties and the gays and lesbians who have successfully linked themselves with women's rights and minority rights organizations.

I felt very uncomfortable as Rusty briefed me. Like many others, I just did not want to hear about these strange goings-on. I like my life simple and sweet and reasonable with an abundance of honesty and love.

Late spring, 1991

Dear Diary,

We have had a terrible accident. Snuf was dozing in the sun in the garage when the overhead door came down on him and broke his neck. He apparently died immediately. He wasn't discovered by my mistress until later. The only explanation is that when my master left the house on an errand he must have activated the overhead door without noticing that Snuf was underneath. Snuf must not have heard the door descending, or did not react if he did hear it. As you might imagine, my master and mistress were quite upset. Snuf had been an important part of the family for about seventeen years and will be missed. My master buried him in the garden next to the pool and planted impatiens to mark his grave. Our little kibbutz has shrunk in size and I feel bad about that. Do you suppose there is a heaven for cats and dogs? I certainly hope so.

I have had another treatment with chemotherapy. I heard the vet tell my master that for the present I will have chemo every six weeks and later on every three months. I guess it is forever, whatever that means. I don't like the prednisone that I am taking. I am always out of breath and my heart beats very fast. My master persuaded the vet to reduce the amount of prednisone, but it doesn't seem to make much difference. But I go along with what my master says.

My master forgot to close the door to the utility room last night. When he came to the kitchen in the morning to take Dutchess and me out, he found I had spread garbage all over the kitchen floor. My only explanation is that the prednisone I am taking makes me very hungry and thirsty and I just could not resist raiding the kitchen. I was scolded but I know he understands the problem and is sympathetic. I know I am testing his patience, just like Melanie does from time to time. But it seems that I have no choice. Melanie may be in the same boat.

I heard someone on TV describe a particularly obnoxious individual as an animal. I resent that. We, animals, have many superior qualities. Take dogs as an example. You can count on our loyalty, we return your love, and we are your protectors. I think we animals should start a PR program to build ourselves a better image and to outlaw the use of the word 'animal' as a derogatory expression.

A few days later, spring, 1991

Dear Diary,

I think my master has caught on that my hearing is not so good anymore. Dutchess and I were out for our morning "necessity." When he called us in for breakfast, I didn't realize he had called until I saw Dutchess whiz past me. When I turned around, I saw him with his hands on his hips. I guessed then that he had called more than once. I wanted to avoid his knowing because he worries so much about me and the princess, Melanie. He doesn't fret about Debbie or Michael anymore. He says that they've got their acts together.

My master took me to the veterinary hospital again this Saturday morning. The tumors on my body have continued to grow despite the fact that I had chemotherapy the beginning of the week. The vet examined me and apparently did not like what he saw and asked my master to bring me back Tuesday for treatment. He said he would administer a new drug.

I am trying to think positively about my cancer. I will overcome it just the way my master did with his cancer seven years ago. He's a great believer in positive thinking. "Nothing can stop the army air corps," he says.

I saw on television last night a ceremony marking the unveiling of the largest American flag commemorating flag day. It measures 400 feet by 200 ft, larger than a football field. It is impressive but I wonder what the government is going to do with it now. You can't fold up something that big and store it away in an attic. I wonder how much it cost. A lot, I bet. I can think of a number of better ways the money could have been spent. Like feeding the hungry. Or finding homes for the homeless. Sometimes I think things like that are done to divert our attention from more important things. Our priorities get screwed up, I am afraid.

Right after the unveiling the TV station showed some pictures of the earth seen from outer space. It was quite dramatic. It looked so remote and peaceful and beautiful. I thought how nice if it were really that way. No famines, no wars, no plagues. Serenely beautiful. Maybe it will be that way one day.

It is interesting that my master keeps a bottle of Aquavit in the freezer. He seldom drinks it. I understand he always kept a bottle in the freezer when his father was alive. His dad liked an occasional schnapps, as he called it. It reminded him of the days when he was a boy and he went to the store in Aalborg, Denmark, to pick up a bottle of Aquavit for his father. A family tradition.

Traditions are an important part of life. They are like sign posts that remind you where you've been and point in the direction that you are likely to travel.

First day of summer, 1991.
Dear Diary,
Today is the first day of summer, I am told. It is the longest day of the year. From now on the days will be getting shorter. I don't like that. For me it is a signal that we are on the downward slope of the year. Summer is my favorite season. The pace of life seems to slow down. There's less rush and there's time to reflect and to feel how good life truly is. I like to sprawl on the deck besides the pool and watch the flowers grow and listen to the summer breezes rustling in the trees and smell the tantalizing fragrances all about me. Summer is a heady concoction, isn't it?

My master took me to the vet a few days ago. It was a nice ride through the countryside. I lay next to him on the passenger side and stretched out so that I could put my head in his lap. He drove with one hand on the wheel and with the other stroked my head. I liked that very much.

I was given a new type of chemo, which seems to be working. My master inspects me regularly and he says the tumors on my body have shrunk. He is very happy. I am, too, believe me. I will be seeing the vet again in a few days to get his opinion on the way the new drug is working.

I have developed an infection on my backside that is unrelated to my cancer. I have tried to treat it by licking it. But that hasn't worked. My licking has only made it worse. I now have a great big collar that I am supposed to wear to keep me from licking. My master puts it on me at night and when they go out. I look kind of silly. It is very big and white. My master says I look like a portrait of Mary, Queen of Scots. I don't like the collar but I am willing to wear it for my own good.

I try not to think about my cancer. My master's advice is to think positively about getting better. He has a routine that goes like this: say to yourself over and over again that the cancer will disappear and that you will get better. It's a form of self-hypnosis that he practised in the early stages of shingles, when the pain was very severe. I am optimistic and yet I am aware that I don't have the strength and vitality I used to have. The vet has told my master to exercise me gently, which means that I should not run and fetch. My master knows how important it is for me not to give in, so he throws the ball just a few times for me to retrieve. I try to do my best and look my best but I am glad when the exercise is done and I can take it easy.

The rest of the family seems to be in good health. The torn rotator cuff in my master's right shoulder has almost completely healed. He is able to swim the crawl now, which he hadn't been able to do for quite a long time. My mistress has less pain in her back and is playing more golf. Deb and Melanie are okay and Mike is able to use his body a little more each day. He has reconciled himself to the fact that he will never regain full use of his back.

When I close my eyes, I can see Heidi and Snuf and we are together again. Our special kibbutz.

Wednesday, June 26, 1991

    I am sorry to report that Peaches' diary entry for the First Day of Summer was her last. She died early this morning as a result of internal hemorrhaging brought on by her last treatment of chemotherapy.

    It has been a dreadful day. She was found this morning at about 6 a.m. in a pool of blood in the laundry room where she and Dutchess sleep. She was still alive but barely. I called the answering service for the animal hospital, told them it was an emergency, and that I was bringing the dog in. I arrived there the same time as a technician. She tried mouth-to-mouth resuscitation, but it was too late. Peaches had expired.

    I was stunned. The vet had examined her only the day before and said that she was reacting positively to the new chemo that had been administered a week earlier. The tumors on her backside and groin had practically vanished. He was enthusiastic about her response and we began planning the next step in her recovery.

    That afternoon she became ill. When I gave her dinner, she threw it up. I saw blood mixed with the undigested food and called the vet. He did not think it was a major problem and prescribed an antacid. She was very listless for the balance of the evening. I was very apprehensive when I turned out the lights around ten and went to bed.

    How I wish that I had gotten up during the night to check on her. If only she had barked or Dutchess had barked. Maybe something could have been done.

    As you can gather from her diary, Peaches was a very important member of our family. She was aptly named. She was a peach of a dog and we are going to miss her terribly. I know she did her best best to survive her battle with cancer and was looking forward to the summer. If there is an Animal Land, I am sure she is there.

Her Master and Editor

A few weeks later.

Peaches is buried in the garden, not far from where Snuf lies. Heidi is buried next to the pond at the house on Main Street, so they are not physically together. I am sure they are together in their kibbutz in Animal Land.

Mike helped me bury Peaches, and he bawled and so did I. Her grave is decorated with yellow lillies and orange impatiens. Snuf's grave is marked with pink impatiens.

Dutchess has tried to be a comfort. She has stuck closeby. I do not know if she understands what has happened. If she does, I am sure she realizes that Peaches is a very hard act to follow. Yet she is there, helping to soften the anguish.

My sorrow has not diminished. Peaches was a great dog, the best, and I counted on her being part of the family for years to come. Maybe that was wishful thinking. Not too many dogs and people survive their battles with cancer. My regret is that I did not awaken during the night when she lay dying. Perhaps I could have done something to help her.

Peaches lived just over nine years. They were good years for her and for the family.

It is a fine line that separates reality from fantasy. In her diary she slipped from one to the other quite easily. Then again who is to say what is reality and what is fantasy. From her point of view they may have been interchangeable.

Her Master and Editor